Lit by
Lightning

⚡

by Nicole Sarrocco

Karate Bride

The Occasionally True Novels

1. Lit by Lightning

2. Ill-Mannered Ghosts
forthcoming February 2016

NICOLE SARROCCO

Lit by Lightning

an Occasionally True
Account of One Girl's Dust-ups
with Ghosts, Electricity,
and Granny's Ashes

⚡

CHATWIN BOOKS
SEATTLE 2015

Cover design by Annie Brulé. Photograph of the author by Jason Hedrick. Edited by Phil Bevis.

This is a work of fiction. No resemblance is intended to any living person, except for kin. Unless you think you recognize yourself—then it's **really** all about you.

paperback ISBN 978-1-63398-000-6

hardcover ISBN 978-1-63398-028-0

Chatwin Books
www.chatwinbooks.com

for my children
all of them
the evening star is rising
it's time to come on inside

CONTENTS

There is always a knock at the door about to happen. The night bends and trembles with the weight of words, the breath of feeling. Every ghost is only a story. You call up a ghost story, looking for its ear. Because even stories never spoken, only thought, are stories born, borne into us as code, unbroken, running like a dog across the snow…

CHAPTER ONE

THOMAS IS MY LAST HUSBAND. You know how when you're
at a potluck and you go get a slice of pie? You really only
intend to have one slice, so you try to pick out a good one.
Sometimes there are real good reasons to go back for another
slice. Like maybe that first one, the one you thought was
homemade chocolate chess pie—turned out to be some store-
bought fraud. Or, I don't know, maybe you're still hungry
after eating the first one. But that third slice—and to be clear,
Thomas is slice #3 for me—definitely has to be your last. So
when I say he is my last husband, I don't mean "latest," I
mean *last*. Past three, and there's words for what you are, and
ain't none of them nice. I'm more certain about this part
than I am about anything else. It's important to know that
from the beginning.

I'm pouring my second cup of coffee, just back inside the
kitchen door from taking Nora to school at 6:30. Earlier, on
the days she has to carry her cello. It's so early for us to get
up, we started getting up fifteen minutes earlier even, so we
can run in circles in the driveway until we wake up. I don't
know if it counts as exercise, but she has math first period
every other day so it's a necessity.

So I'm starting the second phase of morning, making
Edgar's lunch and getting him ready for preschool. He'll ride
to work and stay with me until it's time for his class. Unless
it's Monday. Or Friday. On the days he's the helper, I have
to bring snacks for everybody. It's not his day today. That's
something at least. I might get to bathe before work.

I can tell Thomas is up by looking at the coffee level.
Sometimes Thomas takes Edgar with him to the office, but

this morning he's got a meeting with a client. It helps that we work together. Otherwise, we'd have no food or clean clothes. Possibly the dog would have to watch Edgar on occasion. Or drive a car.

The dog stares up at me as if she's worried about this possibility.

"I've been thinking for a few months about where I'd put my ashes. When I die. A long time from now."

"I sincerely hope you're talking to the dog." It's early, I realize, for this conversation. In all kinds of ways. I hadn't even waited for Thomas to get all the way into the kitchen.

"It's All Souls' Day. Did you hear the knocking at the front door? Last night? About midnight?"

"Since you're ahead of me on the caffeine, how about I catch up."

It's All Souls' Day, the second of November. I just bet you know all about trick-or-treating, the Great Pumpkin, maybe some apple-bobbing in the haunted house. All that stuff, that's All Hallows Eve, right. And a bunch of the really devout still celebrate All Saints Day, the first of November, the day for recognizing those folks who partook of the divine vision but maybe have no declared day of their own. Are there a lot of those? Do you wonder about that? I've kind of wondered. It's pretty freaking hard to get access to the divine vision, but there's only 365 days, so unless somebody shares a day here and there, somebody's getting left out. Who wants to get hold of a divine vision and then have to share a day, really, with somebody like St. Theresa or St. Christopher? Or St. Nicholas? That'd be my luck. It's St. Nicholas's day, and some other person who saw some visions or something.

There's no social failure quite like the ones related to the holidays. The obligations surrounding even the minor festivals are specific and numerous. Right at midnight on the first of November, I heard knocking at my door, like Poe's visitor but with less feathers. I know, because I opened my eyes to look at the clock at 12:01, and by then it had stopped. Four knocks, maybe five. And it wasn't the acorns on the roof. I thought it might be the acorns but they're pretty insistent, and the knocking didn't insist because it was calm and steady. It said we had business, it said, and you know what it is. You know you hear the knocking. You set out a plate for the knocking. You might be in bed doing crossword puzzles. That's cool. We'll come back later.

But back to my social failures for a minute. If you're somebody with unfinished business with the dead, then All Souls' Day ought to be on your calendar. It's November 2nd. Write that down. Leave those skeletons up on your door after the candy's gone and the pumpkin's kicked. They've still got some doings.

How can you tell whether or not you have unfinished business with the dead? Say you have accumulated some human remains, for instance. In your possession. Well, it's not respectful. Or practical. Here's where I've found myself, and knowing full well that All Hallows Eve was coming, I completed a whole series of errands, work projects, returned phone calls and emails without baking a pound cake or even making a half-assed altar. I didn't even call Francis. I always call Francis on All Hallows. Francis is my occult expert and a dear friend, removed by many miles from my presence but not from my daily affection. His chief areas of expertise are Food, Death and Art. There's no better friend to have. Thanks to technology, I still get to benefit from his wisdom regularly.

But I haven't called him yet this year, and now this knocking after midnight, it's already late in this short season. So I'm talking to Thomas about my own ashes, getting it all out of order, making a mess.

"I'm just thinking, you know, where I'd want somebody to put them, I guess I should say. I wouldn't be putting them. Mine, I mean. Anyplace."

Thomas checks his email on his phone. Or so he'd have me believe.

"There's a company in Japan that can make them into pencils. That's my first choice, so far."

I can see his eyebrows moving a little. He'll say something here in a minute.

"I see a drawback to this plan of yours, in that no living member of your family is going to have the slightest interest in owning or using your ash-pencils."

"I don't see why not."

"I'm not making a grocery list with your kneecaps."

"Thomas, if I die, you will be too grieved to eat again."

It's true. I think he's a terror junkie. I think he's become addicted to the chaos.

I'm checking my action list. Post office: check. Clothes in the dryer: check. Orange juice at the store—I'll get that later. I've put a question mark next to "Call Francis." Helpful Heloise would be proud of me on this one: I may not know what to do with the two sets of human remains I'm stuck with at present, but I knew exactly who to call about the Santeria spell in my front yard when that happened, and I knew who to call when the spirits paid me a visit this morning. Come to think of it, Heloise would not be anywhere near this shit.

"Francis. I've got troubles... not of this world. Please call when you can. It's kind of urgent."

Francis isn't home yet. It's not the sort of question you'd leave in a message, but seeing as a time constraint likely applies here, I'm going to do the best I can.

Here's why Francis is the best: one time I had a Santeria spell on my front lawn, and he totally knew how to get rid of it. It threw me at first, and for a few hours I just paced around like a madwoman wondering if I should just hose everything down and forget it, but I figured that acting abruptly and in ignorance could be a mistake. And then I realized that Francis would know exactly what to do.

"So, there's like, a bunch of sugar in my yard. No, in a circle. It's a lot. Like maybe a couple of bags' worth."

It didn't take long, and Francis's instructions were specific. When I told him about the carefully situated pair of ladies' sandals, he rankled: "These people," he sniffed, "have absolutely no idea what they are doing."

"They may not know what they're doing, but I'm going to need some peace of mind here. What do you suggest?"

Some fascinating side notes to this incident: it turns out you have to go up to the counter at the Mexican grocery and ask for Agua Florida, a key element in overturning what Francis called the "sweetening spell" that may or may not be working on me. In fact, the cashier may disappear for a moment, but he'll be back. Buy a candle or a sweet biscuit or something if you want to feel less weird about the whole transaction.

"The point is," Francis warned me, "you don't even want anyone thinking they're working you. Even if they're doing it wrong." I did like the smell of the stuff, and I also came very close to remembering the Lord's Prayer without having to look it up on my phone. But since you don't want to screw up the antidote to a half-assed Santeria spell out of bravado, I looked that shit up, and I got it right. Then I used the kitchen matches to light the Agua Florida and set my front stoop stones on fire.

"Watch the flames. There will be some blue ones in the center, and that's normal. You just don't want any spirals. If the flames spiral, I'm going to give you some further instructions. Don't worry." No spirals. So I think we're clear of that, whatever it was.

$$\frac{}{}$$

Wallace Stevens said one time that life is an affair of people, not places, but for him life was an affair of places and that was the trouble. That's trouble, yes it is. My life is an affair of places who are like people.

"If the afterlife is the most peaceful thing you can imagine, I guess I think maybe it's a dogsled. Do you think scattering ashes from a dogsled would be a good thing? Would that be sufficiently respectful?"

"Did you have a particularly difficult therapy session yesterday?" Thomas takes a long sip of coffee, staring at me. "It's a hard decision—I don't know what I'd do if I had the same problem. And I didn't know your grandmother, so it's hard for me to say what she'd want. I know she's not, well, bothering you like she was before, but having her sitting there in the dining room—it may be okay for her, but it seems like it's not okay for you."

Francis knew right what to do about the Santeria spell. I'm going to ask him about the ashes. As soon as I can get in touch, but there's a lot to get done today.

"And you know me. I don't care. She can stay. I'm just saying. Seems like it's wearing you out a little bit."

Dogsledding may sound like a strange image of the afterlife to you, but let me explain. The most non-personally exhilarated I have ever been was the one time I got to be on a dogsled. Staring at the stars. Hearing nothing but the dogs' panting. Their feet crushing the snow, soft little crackles.

I'd miss the dogs' panting, after they dumped me and left. I don't really want to be left on a glacier, come to think of it. How often would the dogs run by? Getting out to a glacier would be impractical, too.

What's more impractical than death? Man, when I moved from Seattle, I found out just how impractical it could be when I had to ship that urnful of my closest relative back to North Carolina.

"Contents of package..."

I'm at my friendly neighborhood Pack and Ship, trying to ship Granny's ashes back to North Carolina. I was moving home, so she was, too. Post 9/11, and you can't just take a sealed metal box on the plane and sit with it in your lap. So I'm talking to the same nice man who helped me get my dissertation printed and shipped a few months back. He wants to know, naturally, what's in the box.

"Well, see... contents. The contents are, this box is the...

the contents. Ashes. Remains. IS technically what... that's...
Granny."

My babbling began to make some kind of sense to him,
because he put his pencil down and ran his hand quickly back
and forth through his curly hair. Kind of like he was looking
for the source of a diffuse itch. Then he turned around really
fast, walked away and into the back room for a second, then
came back out to the counter and picked up his pencil and
clipboard.

"Okay. We're going to start again, and here's how it's going to go. I'm going to pretend I didn't hear what you just
told me. Name, yes, contact phone number, delivery zip and
yes, check, yes, and contents. Contents: Yes. All right. Contents: one art object."

He glanced up at me sidelong.

"Value of contents—"

Now he really shot me a look, and went back to scrawling
in a kind of cramped, perturbed fashion as he pronounced
each syllable and scrawled one word onto the form.

"Ir-re-place-a-ble."

"I can't take her on the plane," I offered.

He just glanced up again and sighed.

"No, I guess you can't. This is disrespectful." He shook his
head again, slower this time.

"Yeah. I fully expect to pay. And I don't just mean for the
shipping."

Remembering it all there in my kitchen, I'm staring down

into Edgar's lunchbox I've been absent-mindedly packing. Edgar stands at the bottom of the stairs in his baggy Star Wars pajamas, disheveled from heavy sleep. I realize that I'm still paying, and that's part of all of this. There is a debt I have. We all have to do our best with these things. Some are more complicated than others.

"Hey there, little man. Did you have nice dreams?" Thomas walks over and sweeps Edgar into his arms. Edgar giggles.

What if it's all just out there, in the air?

"What if what's all out there? In the air." I guess I asked that question out loud.

"All of the stuff. The things they didn't finish. All of the things we didn't finish with them. Everybody's stories. The air could be full of them, you know. Like invisible tumbleweeds, catching on real live people sometimes, following them around like ghost clouds. Word ghosts. Ghost parables. What if we're stuck all over with stories that flew out of people when they died?"

"Oh, it's all out there. That's exactly where it is." He rubs noses with Edgar.

"I think about things," said Edgar.

If I only had one ash problem, that would be one thing. It's never one thing.

"What you're talking about is conservation of energy—if you're interested in an explanation." And this is why I ask Thomas stuff. Listening to Thomas's explanations gives me the same feeling as dumping out the necklaces in my jewelry box and untangling them with the tweezers.

"You mean if something's not right on this side..."

"It's got to balance. It's an irrefutable rule of nature." I wonder if I'd be that calm and confident if I smoked.

↯

You'll dream about my damp hair against your cheek tonight, and you will think of someone in your world. But it's really me. I've always been here. I'm going to start running tonight, and I won't stop until I reach you. I will have to forget everything and remember all over again, and so will you. But I won't stop. I don't know what this place is, but I won't stop. Here comes the snow.

CHAPTER TWO

THE MOST IMPRACTICAL THING, besides death, would be ex-husbands. I have to call Brad, because the other set of ashes I'm worried about is another story. I don't even know exactly where they are. There. I said it. I don't know. That was the first thing I had to admit, before I could even start to put this whole thing in order. I don't know who has my son's ashes. If anybody does. I do know one place they are not, and that's as far as I've gotten. It's hard. That part you probably believe.

In the car, I'm practicing the speech I would make. And by practicing, I mean I'm saying it to him, because he's there, my son who died. It's going to be really hard to believe, this next part, but just hang in there with me. It's going to be kind of like at the beginning of the movie Evita, when Antonio Banderas opens his mouth to sing, and you've got to decide right then whether you're going to take this trip with him. You've got to think: Antonio Banderas is singing, and I kind of don't believe it, but he's probably going to sing again in the next two hours, so let's just go along and see what happens. I'm going to tell you more than once that when you have some business with somebody on the other side, they are around. So if I'm wrong and you're right, then maybe I am only rehearsing, or I'm repeating myself for consolation. Like a nursery rhyme. Or a prayer. And that's not hurting anybody, is it?

"I am pretty sure your ashes are in a filing cabinet, and I am just chagrined about that. I can't tell you how much I am. I am trying to get this mess worked out. The truth is, until recently I thought they were under a monkey puzzle tree in a remote area near the Canadian border, so this is better, potentially. I know the next series of decisions needs to be carefully considered. Sorry it's taking so long. I know you must have been wondering what was up with me."

Here's how the first conversation with Brad went. "I hear you're selling the house in Darien." That's how I started, because his house was the last place I knew where they were.

"Yes. Yes, that's happening. The paperwork's going through and everything. I have to go out there and get the stuff out next month—the people seem nice and it's a second home—"

"You selling it with the dead guy's towels? Gonna include those?" The dead guy was the guy who owned the house before Brad's family. I always called him "the dead guy." That's another story I'll get to in a minute.

"Probably."

"You should throw those out. But that's not why I called."

I don't know why I offer suggestions for normal behavior now, when he never took any of them when we were married. Or when we were kids.

"Brad, I really just have a short question, and I'm sorry to bring this up, but I need to know. If I can just get this answer today. Then we can discuss it further later."

And so it turned out that nobody ever put those ashes under the monkey puzzle tree, even though that's what Brad's mother had said. The whole story about scattering my son's ashes in Darien had just come out of the old lady's imagination.

I won't miss the house itself. It was pretty regular, on the scale of things. Sad. Kind of flat and sad. With some Southwest-inspired design choices that I guess somebody thought made it look rustic. Maybe they just conflated Northwest and Southwest. That's kind of sad, because they are totally differ-ent things. It's like building a Swiss chalet in Portugal. Who am I kidding. Somebody's probably done that. People are not places, and places don't get their feelings hurt.

Anyway, that place was freaking lonely, and not just be-cause driving down that road at night made you feel like you were doing a historical re-enactment of *In Cold Blood.* I know it never bothered Brad's family, living in a house a guy died in. The Henrys cheerfully used the dead guy's towels, slept soundly on his mattress. That's some real shit, right there. Sleeping on the mattress. I have to give it to them on that one. If you're going to live in a death house, sleep on the death mattress. I think whatever was left of that guy watched Brad's father Victor open up his can of pork and beans and set it up there on top of the pilot light to warm while he went out with his stick and bells to talk to the bears on Mt. Higgins, with that dead guy thinking the whole time, Man, fucking congratulations. You're the full realization of the modern, dude. You are the *now.*

We had to stay in the house when we first moved out to the Pacific Northwest, before we bought a place in Seattle. One day, just out of the shower, I was staring at an Yves St. Laurent stripey number circa 1978, asking myself if Brad's mother would have moved these things across the country to her summer cottage.

"This towel."

"Yeah?"

"This the dead guy's towel?"

Brad just sighed.

"You brought me out here to the middle of nowhere to
dry off with dead people's towels? Where your parents sleep
on a dead guy's mattress? What are we eating with? How old
are the light bulbs? The canned goods? We're one clown away
from Stephen King out here. I'm looking for CROATAN
carved underneath the fucking kitchen table!"

For years, they laughed at me for insisting there was a Sas-
quatch out in those woods. Then they found him. An ancient
hippie dude—living, mind you, in case all the woo-woo stuff
doesn't freak you out like it does me—who was living in a cave,
breaking into houses, stealing food from people's pantries
and rearranging the furniture. Like the Bigfoot branch of
the Manson clan. I mean, I think the light bulbs were a valid
question. They were the only things between me and the dark.

But this particular dead guy seemed amenable enough.
Only the living people in that house were seriously out to
hurt anything. The Henrys on their summer sojourn. I imagined they had been given some guidelines or instructions—at
least, they all did know what had just happened, so I expected
things to be... I guess I expected maybe some level of sensitiv-
ity that didn't exactly emerge. Brad left me alone with them
for a few weeks right after our son died. He later confessed
that the whole thing had been an experiment to see if I could
withstand extended periods of time with them.

"I'm calling from outside the Earl Scheib auto shop. In
Arlington, yes. We came into town to get something on the
truck fixed. I don't know where they all are. I'm here with
Victor and the truck. They went someplace on foot. I turned
around and they were all gone. Yes, I'm alone here. Well,
with Victor."

Victor was reading *Guns, Germs, and Steel.* He looked pretty pissed. He did just have to pay for a car repair, though, and nothing put the man in a worse humor than picking up the check. Brad was in LA making a movie about pornography. He thought it would be good for me to spend time with his family, since they mostly knew me as "Brad's new girlfriend who showed up pregnant." With a round piece of vintage luggage that seemed to indicate to them a character flaw I never was able to identify. Prissy, they said. I also think a couple of them lost money on betting whether Brad was gay. To say their imaginations were limited gives them credit for resources far outside their available scope.

"I'm not fucking kidding. I need you to get me out. Can't you send somebody out here with a plane ticket?"

It was going to be another week before a break in shooting. He was coming up to get me then. I was heading to spend the rest of the summer in a production office full of porn stars. Our son had died two weeks before.

"Your sister burst into my room last night and asked me what the hell was wrong with me."

I ran out of quarters. I couldn't get Victor's attention away from the arresting Mr. Diamond.

I wheeled back around to the phone. "Happy Motherfucking Fourth of July, fuckstick. Your family fucking sucks, and I hate you," I whispered hard into the receiver and slammed it down.

But the rest of them were wandering back, in pieces. The teenager, the old woman, the sister/daughter and the Imp. There weren't enough seats in the truck for everyone, so they put me sideways in the cargo area. The Imp had to ride in the front seat, for reasons neither medical, legal or, as it seemed, negotiable.

"Um, hello. Can someone tell me what the liquid is back here? Because there's liquid spilling from under the tarps, and I can't see what it is."

Victor usually kept some extra gas in the truck, but I was hoping maybe somebody had chucked a water bottle back here. Or a Coke, or something.

"I'm not upset, but if you could just maybe let me know if whatever it is might be flammable."

The sister/daughter and the teenager laughed really hard. It wasn't until later that I found out that it was a jar of the Imp's pee she was carrying home to measure. She kept a journal of weights and volumes.

After more errands than seemed possible on a national holiday in the Northwest equivalent of Dogpatch, Victor and I were left alone again at the Armory, waiting for the fireworks. The others had gone off looking for food. Or human sacrifice candidates. Or containers for bodily fluids.

Victor was talking about the navy. Maybe it was a patriotism thing, bunting and flags everywhere, kids running around with stars on their shirts. "On the aircraft carrier, you couldn't sit up in bed," he kept saying. About how the bunks were stacked, three maybe four guys stacked up. "Like we were in graves," he said. "You couldn't sit up—you'd hit the guy on top of you. Guy pissed his bed once. Pee started raining on me. Gaahhhd! Stacked up three maybe four guys. You didn't have any room. No privacy."

"Did you ever get scared?" The truth was, I liked Victor. I can't tell you how many men I've judged based on their fathers who actually turned out to be more like their mothers. Lord have mercy on anyone making this common mistake.

"Whaddaya mean? Huh. Yeah." Like it was obvious. But not like I was stupid. Like it was a relief.

The fireworks started before they got back, which was good, because then nobody talked.

After our beautiful, healthy daughter Nora was born Brad quit leaving the house for anything but hardware. There were a lot of trips to Lowes for extension cords and lightbulbs, but he never worked again, which sucked on the money front and on the sanity front. In one attempt to hit some kind of reset button, our couples therapist asked Brad what he had seen in me, in the beginning. What the most important thing about me was. What he most appreciated about me. And he said I was a brat, that he liked that I was a brat. That was all he had, bratdom. And that was the end of discussion. The case closed.

"The two things I don't want to hear about this Christmas: your play, and your hair." That was the last thing he said to me as a husband. On a plane. At the beginning of our long flight home to our families. I think I might have been able to win him over if I'd had the wherewithal to turn around, look him in the eye and say, "Where exactly are our baby's ashes, you sentimental goat?" But from that moment on, in my mind, it was over.

My life is an affair of places. Of people-places.

I think the very last time I was in the dead guy's house, the Henrys were squabbling over who would be forced to take Victor to Riverdance. "He says he wants to go. He says it's the last form of art he can appreciate." Gladys was pushing, but nobody in that selfish tribe would suck it up and volunteer.

"It's the last art form left I can appreciate," he complained, and while I didn't understand what the fuck he meant exactly, it sure sounded serious.

"I SAID THAT ALREADY. He can't hear," Gladys shouted at him over the electric can opener. She was working her way through multiple cans of fishy cat food.

The man warmed beans on a pilot light to save power and still remembered getting peed on in an aircraft carrier barracks. The only things I had ever heard him express much affection toward were velour shirts and Riverdance.

"Hell, I'll take him," I heard myself say.

"Thanks. Ahem-erm," Victor said, clearing his throat snidely and turning back to the newspaper. He can hear, I thought. What do you know. But he's got a hairball.

I dressed up; he wore a cardigan that still had elbows. The production was a spectacle, and the bullhorn, jackhammer clackity-clackity-clack of shoes assaulted even my Black Flag-trained ears, but Victor, sans hearing aid, sat back and smiled contentedly. Later, in the narrative bridge scene, when the patented Riverdance clackity-clackity dance-step sound had dissipated for some romantic Spanish guitar, Victor turned to me and said confidentially, "They've got the quiet shoes on now."

It was years later, Victor long gone from my life, that I stood outside that same theater, the Paramount on lower Capitol Hill in Seattle, remembering the pathos of quiet shoes as I stood witnessing what for me became my lasting symbol of pointless and ignominious death: a man run down in the street while leaving the theater after the Friday evening performance of *Mamma Mia*.

I myself was skittering home after a performance of something I'd written for a cabaret theater down the street. This was nothing to handle alone. I did as I often do when the darkness peers into me: I took out my phone and called Francis.

"I have to tell you what I'm seeing here."

"I hear sirens! Are you okay?"

I gave a brief overview.

"Oh, dear. That's positively one of the most awful deaths I can imagine for anyone. Was it after the first or second act?"

"That's a good question. I can't tell much from here—I'm trying to keep my distance."

"I don't suppose you've got any holy water in your bag."

"No. I have lipstick and Advil and three bucks and a driver's license. And Altoids. And a paperclip."

I stood on the street corner and watched the ambulances and fire trucks, the police, the crowds on the sidewalk who also had just attended Mamma Mia but for whom additional life experiences lay in wait to temper whatever way that two hours had affected them, plus or minus.

"People should not die with images of multicolor bell-bottom pants and feather boas lingering on their retinas." Francis was firm on this.

"This kind of makes my heart hurt, but do you think he might have been running from the theater in distress and horror, à la *Rites of Spring*?" Where were his loved ones? No one at this scene was acting like loved ones. What would I be doing if this man belonged to me?

Blinded by the neon, disoriented by earsplitting pop harmonies and Rachmaninoff runs, the poor man must have looked across the street and seen The Cloud Room atop the decaying Camlin Hotel and bolted thither for safety. I was considering The Cloud Room myself, standing alone opposite the most concentrated shameful sorrow I could imagine. A few floors up, there were cheap Old Fashioneds and a man playing hits of the '70s on an electric piano. From the balcony, you could see the whole city in a much more detached, manageable form than it ever seemed to be from street level.

"You should definitely go on up to The Cloud Room, honey. Have one for me. I'd meet you there, but I'm in for the evening."

"Francis, don't hang up. What should I do? His whole life is probably out here, floating down Pine Street. That's no way to end. I feel like I need to go catch it in a net."

"You have to let that go for now. It's not yours. You know that gypsy saying: not my circus, not my monkeys."

"Francis, the Paramount's got some lights out in the marquee. Underneath 'Mamma Mia! Ends Tonight!' it just says 'Tick, Tick' instead of 'Ticket Ticket.'"

"Oh, honey. Erase all of this from your memory."

This place is cold, and it's moving so fast. It's freezing me from the inside out when I try to breathe—but my face feels warm and my arms feel warm—I can't exactly feel my arms and legs, but everything else is warm. Except the cold coming in. And I can hear these things chasing me. Big things. They must be close because I can hear them breathing now, breathing in that cold cold air. Are they getting closer?

CHAPTER THREE

IT'S NOT THAT THE PRESENCE of disembodied spirits in or
around the house is any kind of deal-breaker. There's just
not enough instructional material available for handling this
shit.

Francis has now left me a message in response to my current message. It's a short one. I'll get to it in a minute.

The man in our new house is sad, but he's harmless. He
comes up behind me in the kitchen, especially when I'm
standing over in the corner between the stove and the wall
oven, often when I'm at the blender. Maybe there was something else there in the first house, the little one that got
expanded into the lovely rambling Frankenstein floor plan of
the current house. The electrics are funky in that corner; the
lights flicker at me. He comes over though when I'm there.
He just wants me to remember that it was his house. He built
it, that main part. It was his. There was dark paneling, but
one of the later owners took it out—maybe like a knotty pine
or something, but he liked it. He liked boats. I'm not sure
if he had one, but I think maybe. We're pretty close to Lake
Wheeler. I think he had a boat, like a sport one, for waterski-
ing.

I waterskied once. Lake Geneva, Florida, lumpy with its
nubby alligators—we went every summer, and that especial
summer my dad determined I would put down my book and
learn to ski. After a couple of hours of wrestling, swearing,
fearful fake alligator or snake sightings, and mighty com-
plaints, I made it one time around the lake without falling.
As I saw the little beach by our cabin roll into view, I let go.
It was worth all the struggle for those few seconds, sailing

forward over the water standing up, no boat, no line, barely hearing my father's stupid disbelieving insults over the motor WHAT DO YOU THINK YOU'RE DOING as I flew like fucking Winged Victory to the shore. Like a fat Winged Victory in a Bicentennial bathing suit. But the wind blew my wet hair straight back and up, like a fire, and my wooden feet slid with a satisfied crunch into the sand. I walked out of the rubber shoes and off, back to the clap of the screen door.

This man in the new house, he's all right. He never hurt anybody. He just wants you to remember that it was his house. He was proud of it.

There was a man in the old house, too. He used to try to scare me when I did the laundry, but that was just because nobody was allowed in the basement when he was there. DON'T come down here, he'd say. My TOOLS are down here. Let me KNOW if you have to come down here. He really didn't mean any harm either, he just had stuff, you know, stuff he didn't want anyone to see. I didn't want to see it either, and I told him so one night.

"Look," I said at the bottom of the crappy carpeted stairs, "Whatever it is, I don't care. I've got laundry. I don't care what you're doing. You do your business and I'll do mine—but don't move shit and don't show me anything. I know you're here. Just go about it."

When we built Thomas's recording studio, it was right in the middle of the tool man's domain. I guess I kind of lied to him. But he didn't get angry—I don't know. He turned away. He got confused about where he was. And then one day, I didn't feel him at all anymore.

"You didn't think to mention it in the, what, four years we lived there?" Thomas asked me.

"Hey, new husband, the invisible cranky old man in the basement is sad because your rock and roll music crap is all up in his tools."

We talked about the old man in the basement one day—the day my, let's say, observations first really became a conversational topic. We were watching some kind of freaky haunted house show, and the gadget-toting ghost hunters called some woman who "read" spaces—she comes in and sniffs around and starts talking about the feelings in the house.

"Zuleika Hobstobble is a sentient medium," the ghost hunters say. I don't think "sentient medium" is even a term. Some kind of medium, whatever it was they said, meant she could pick up on feelings in places.

"Pfth. Everybody can do that." I snorted at the TV, wondering what the point was going to be if she couldn't come up with some times and dates. I was also wondering if she was managing some fiscal remunerations out of this little endeavor.

"Can do... ah, no. No, I don't sense shit when I walk into an old house. Not unless something stinks."

"Come on. You know if something really fucked-up happened. That's why you have to walk around in a place before you move in. I usually lie down on the floor of the bedroom. Better safe than sorry."

"Let me get this straight: previously, rental and real estate agents have watched you without comment while you lie down on the floor in the bedroom?"

"I would imagine they respect my forethought. What are you going to do if you get into a place and there's static and fizzling in the bedroom? And you can't sleep?"

"You don't sleep!"

"That's why it's so important that nothing interrupts it when I do! That crackle crackle—I hate that."

"I have no fucking idea. None."

"You do, you just don't think about it."

"No. Categorically. This might explain a lot. Your giant antenna—it's not just picking up people."

For a straight-up facts kinda guy, Thomas has been all over this. It's simple, for him. I've got details I couldn't have any other way, and I'm crazy, like, pushy and unpleasant—but not delusional-crazy. So we're open to options. He took me to a place he knew from childhood, a doctor's house. When I told him about the doctor's daughter standing under the scup-pernong grape arbor—and her little cat—it's been easier since then, really. This case is not closed.

The cabin in Florida had a man in it, too. Do-it-yourself-ers, they hang around. When they've built on the place, when they swing the hammers into the walls, when they pull out the wires and put them back, the veins of the house, they're in the blood, in the dirt. They don't leave.

↯

Sometimes it seems like they are right up beside me in the dark, but they can't catch me. I'm moving very fast; I'm not sure how. I thought I was running. It feels like running. Why can't I see them? Just some flecks of fur that brush my cheek, and the rest is dark. Please devour me. Please just go ahead and eat me. I can't keep running like this forever.

CHAPTER FOUR

Do you blow up light bulbs?" I'm talking to Soren. He's a psychic.

"Blow light bulbs? Oh no. I don't do that. It'd be kind of cool, though. Do you blow up light bulbs?" I'm riveted. Soren's an Icelandic pixie psychic I met through a friend, and he's been asking me all about my experiences. Whether or not I see them, you know. The spirits. We're onto questions of lighting now, evidently.

"So you never saw any entities? Even when you were young—sometimes, it's too much. When we get older, we just…".

Shut them out, I thought to myself. We don't accept them. I used to tell them, "just don't let me see you…".

But I might have. I might have, but I don't think about it.

"And smells—how about those? Do you notice unusual ones? Things other people don't?"

I used to smell oranges and tobacco at this one friend's house. The old man. Old man, I'd say, I'm coming around this corner. Get your business done.

Soren is talking. I can't get over how happy it makes me, hearing about somebody else's—well, issues. Like old ladies in a waiting room, talking about their prescriptions and in-laws. "Me, I blow light bulbs all the time," he says. "It's energy, you know, it pulls the energy. They don't go BOOM, you know, they just burn out like, every month I have to buy so many light bulbs…".

Thomas comes around the corner with a new pack of ciga-rettes, shaking it with a flick. "Light bulbs? She blows them.

It's the damnedest thing. Is that a thing? Y'all blow up light bulbs? Good to know. I already started buying cases."

Soren smiled a big smile at me. "See, you say you don't see things. You don't. You don't know what you see."

"Well, how long is a light bulb supposed to last, like regularly? Don't they last about a month?"

"In this house, but not for most people," Thomas says. "I just replaced all the bulbs in the hallway last week, and we've only got two left. Your closet—Jesus, you must be so pissed when you're getting dressed in the morning. I don't even replace them one at a time anymore. I can't keep up. I wait until there's about ten at a time. Last weekend? That was twelve."

I'm on Ancestry.com and Findagrave.com all the time these days. I have a whole bunch of our family's graves across piedmont North Carolina mapped out, and Nora and I go with our cameras. We've taken a lot of pictures, but I don't see any orbs. To be fair, I haven't really looked at the pictures. Maybe a couple on the camera. But I haven't downloaded any of them. I think Nora has. People are buried, lots of them, and it's settled. Maybe I should inter the ashes—you can still do that in a cemetery. I need to quit pretending it's like booking a hotel room. The trip is over.

I don't know about orbs. Would you be an orb? I don't find them all that compelling. They move like carnival rides, and I don't enjoy that. Maybe if you're a different kind of matter, that kind of abrupt jerking around is more entertaining. But it looks like a bad ride on the Scrambler to me. And a bubble. I'd prefer not to be a bubble. There's got to be something more dignified. There's the misty mass—I don't know how I feel about a misty mass. Unsatisfied. I'd feel ungroomed. I think I'd like to take possession of an inanimate object. That's fucking scary, though. Maybe if I can work it out with everybody ahead of time, it could be kind of cool in a *Bedknobs and Broomsticks* kind of way.

I leave Granny's coffee pot by her urn. I'd love to see the coffee pot just start spinning, like I hit it in a shooting gallery. She won't play that way, though. She moves my hairbrush, won't let my car start. I want to say, Why don't you just get in the coffeepot and then we could talk? She tells me I am being too dramatic, that this is all me. She says I need to let her go. It's my fault she's here. Where else are you going, I think. It took you two full days to get dressed for the grocery store. Your preparations for the afterlife must be positively scandalous in proportion.

"Soren asked me if I see stuff. I told him no, but when I was a kid, I used to talk to the things when I knew they were there."

"Well, sure." Francis knows what I mean. That's why I'm talking to him. "You told them things?"

"I'd say 'I don't want to see you' in the barn, or in the bathroom. I always turned over the mirror in my own room, so I wouldn't see things in it. I think it takes a lot out of them to show up, so they may as well save their strength and not give me a heart attack."

"You're right. It's an effort for them. Maybe that's why it scares you—you're sensing their stress, like you do anybody else's."

"I didn't mention this to Soren—I don't know why—but I did just see somebody for the first time in years. It was only a few weeks ago. I've been racking my brain, and I've got nothing. I don't know who she was. A gray dress, 1930s era probably. Modigliani face and a bun. She wasn't attached to the house. She came to me. But I'm not sure I know her."

Most nights I don't sleep between about 3 and 5, and she rolled in about 3:15 and sat down on the edge of the bed. This is some kind of bad news, I thought. I couldn't move. My dog Toast was curled up on the end of the bed, chasing rabbits in her sleep. The lady kind of smiled at me, which freaked me out even more, because a smile from an un-known, semi-transparent entity sitting on the edge of your bed at 3 a.m. falls outside of social discourse. I grew up with a lot of rules for social discourse. We've had to host a lot of problematic people in the South. We've built a culture on how to absorb the inappropriate. If I was, say, still in posses-sion of her cake plate from the bake sale, I'd know what to say to her. I can't for the life of me remember any rules, how-ever, that govern conversations with dead strangers, so I can only resort to the ones that address communicating with liv-ing strangers. In your bedroom. I can't think about much at all except to wonder why it is I'm not screaming. In my head, of course, I'm thinking, Thomas, wake up, because you need to see the shit that is going down here, seriously.

Then, like a freaking horror movie that I won't watch, except in this case I can't plug my ears and shut my eyes and sing "Stars and Stripes Forever," she starts to bend down like she's going to kiss me on the cheek. Instead, she whispers in my ear, "Your children are fine." Then she sits back up and smiles. It's kind of like my ex-mother-in-law's passive-aggressive I-just-trumped-your-ass smile. Not good. I don't like it.

"Honey, they get lost like the rest of us. And sometimes, they're just crazy."

That's what Francis told me when I called to tell him about the freaky Modigliani lady. They get lost. They're in the wrong place.

I don't know why I waited so long to ask, but it's a relief at least to know that my son's ashes aren't under the monkey puzzle tree at my ex-in-laws' ex-house. I have hypothetically told myself that it doesn't matter. Maybe it would have done me a favor, the decision made and not really reversible. What would I have done? Put up a marker? What about the new people? Would I have knocked on their door? What would I have told them?

"My son's ashes are fertilizing this succulent. By the way, I'd buy a new mattress if I were you."

So here's what I say to my son again: This plan doesn't begin with me retrieving ashes from the filing cabinet. That's what I've been building toward—I wish it didn't sound like a dodge, but there are some things I have to have straight before I carry you in my arms again. Do you remember the UNC library? I was doing dissertation research when I got pregnant, and I always thought you liked the library. Maybe it was the chairs. You remember how we talked a lot when I was in the reference room, writing down call numbers from those old oblong green numbers and letters.

Nobody says anything helpful when you die. "Sorry, Hey. Sorry about... you know... that thing." That's what Brad's boss had said over the phone. I wish I had told him that it helped. In its ineloquence, it was by far inadvertently the smartest thing anybody offered. But then people say such unbelievable stuff. I can still remember the sound of his voice on the line, begging for the mercy of my interruption.

"Thanks. Yeah. I know. Um, thanks."

You know there are sounds humans can't usually make. We're not made for mourning. We're animals. There is a sorrow past our evolution. We can't make its sound unless something comes through us like a current, a dark lightning, pain that comes out in a sound. You ever put a cat in a bathtub and wonder what happens to it? It thinks you're killing it. It sees death coming and it's telling you about it. Describing it in detail.

I burn a lot of sage, like Francis suggested. It makes me feel proactive. I know what delusion smells like. It's woody and green. Every alarm is a false one, in the end.

↯

Not getting closer—no, they are pulling me along. They're panting hard. I think I see it, their puffs of breath. I think I can see it like the clouds. It's dark but I can see the clouds between the stars. The stars... they are everywhere.

CHAPTER FIVE

"WE NEED THE SQUIRRELLER. Get the squirrel. I got it." He sighs and crawls down off the stool. He finds the beaters for the electric mixer in the drawer and gets out some blue chopsticks, too.

My son Edgar can separate an egg, even though he's only three—he was born able to crack eggs as if he had a species adaptation. He still hasn't completely mastered crayon technique, but he can assemble a shell-free bowl of egg whites. Baking is chemical. It's real.

"Don't need those," I tell him, but he isn't convinced, and he loves a kitchen utensil like some kids love Legos.

"Oh yes. We do."

Cooking with Edgar reminds me of cooking with my uncle Nick. Old Italian men sigh a lot, too. We watch the pound cake through the steamy oven window, Edgar on the stool, leaning just enough forward to balance himself against the oven door with the tips of his fingers.

"Here it comes. It's going up and up, and it keep up and up until it goes POOOFFF! PPOOMMMA! It gonna get really, really big and we have to watch it. We watching it. You watch it, and I watch it. And the man watch it. The man watch us, too. The man is, is, is a sign."

Characters come and go in Edgar's conversations. Like with most kids his age. Sometimes not exactly like most kids his age. "The man has a sign?"

"Nope. He IS a sign."

Edgar's got the kind of unshakeable confidence that makes

some people think children can access some kind of chthonic wisdom. (Are you one of those people who think big words sound funny in a Southern accent? We're still using doilies down here. We like fancy.) Why is it parents either don't listen at all or listen way too much? A lot comes out, and some of it sounds like something you've heard before. Or want to hear. You're listening to a radio full of static, fiddling with the dials and trying to ask it questions. They're little fleshy Ouija boards.

"Is the man okay?"

"He's okay."

"Does he want anything?" Besides the squirreller, because clearly that's not optional. I'm along for the ride here.

"Yeah. He wants something."

"Does he want us to do something?"

Edgar stops and thinks. "He wants us to watch."

I remember the poet Yeats and his young wife, huddled up in a chilly tower in the dark West of Ireland. Yeats was so caught up in his eclectic devotion, his homemade mysticism, and he wanted his bride to be a part of it, of course. So he decided her fire-like mind would attract the stories from the Other Side. She was not as simple as he imagined, and when winter set in, she delivered the stories that would induce her husband to move to cozier confines: "The spirits say it's too cold to talk. The spirits would like to go to the city."

So I go ahead and ask what he wants us to watch. Knowing that it might be the squirreller. Or Sesame Street.

"Watch. Just watch."

Every alarm is a false one.

My children feel things. Edgar talks to animals and...
other things. Nora's a divining rod for sorrow, but I don't
think she knows it. At first it was just her friend Ian, and I
didn't think much about it, just that it was a coincidence. Or
I figured that Nora found something familiar in him, especially after I met his mother. She renovated old houses. Every
time I saw her she had on a flannel shirt and work boots. She
hadn't slept much in years, either. We only talked about it
once, and she said I heard about your son, and I said I heard
about your daughter. We sat for a while in her old 1978 Mercedes, a bear of a car, looking out the window at First Avenue,
people crossing in the street, all of them unaware of how close
they were to being nothing. One bus. One manhole. One
loose piece of Skylab, ending its forty-year ambling descent
on your noggin. "You can't tell people," she said. "You can't
tell." Before she heaved the Mercedes back into traffic, she
looked up at me. "I have to have a car like this. Otherwise I
couldn't drive at all."

So Ian, that made some sense. But then there was Jacob.
We went to pick her up from his birthday party and I saw his
mother in another room of the house, her gray sweater high
around her neck, hugging herself. I could see it on her like a
tattoo.

"Something's up with Jacob's mother."

And Brad said, "They lost a child. Didn't I tell you?"

"Jacob's older sister."

"Yes. I think it was an illness." Brad was picking some cat
fur off of his fleece.

"Good to find this out on the doorstep. Thanks for nothing."

I'd study them, riding their bikes around the oval in the park off Jackson. Ian rode fast, and so did Nora—she rode the school tricycle off the pre-kindergarten trailer's deck, full speed, and then they called her "Motocross Girl" for the rest of the year. Her teacher said, "I was all the way across the playground, and I saw her decide. By the time I got there, she was in the air. But she tucked and rolled like a champ. Where'd you learn that, Nora?"

She and Ian put their bikes in the car. In the back seat, they tell each other knock-knock jokes, and the only punch line is "poop." The only difference is the way you say it each time. But it's always funny.

Jacob was different. I don't think I ever heard Jacob speak. He wore tights and had never had a haircut. He reminded me of a tiny Henry Rollins, circa 1983, crouched on the arm of a sofa growling poetry and sniffing the punk rock kids in the Ashe Avenue house. If Jacob knew any poems, he just whispered them to Nora. She would nod for a while, then she'd say, Hush now. Okay. Okay.

What was he whispering? Something like: "Do you remember what it was like? Living in a dead person's room? You have the same blood. Your heart memorized beating in there by listening to the echoes of his. You closed up your gills and learned about being a person because he told you that's what you had to do. That you couldn't stay in there. What did he tell you before you came here?"

Hush now.

"She told me we can't stay here either. It's just another little room with the echoes of dead people's hearts beating in it. Can you hear them? I think I can."

⚡

Thomas comes in from the porch, putting out the small fire of his cigarette. "I'm beat. The vault at the office set off another false alarm at 5:30 this morning."

I know, I said. False alarm.

"I just sent another angry email to LockDown. I swear, at this point, if we blow up like the fourth of July, the Raleigh Fire Department is not coming. You watch."

He was my first child, the son Brad and I lost. He died on the same day of the year that Brad first kissed me, back in high school. I think it was the universe saying, "In the history of bad ideas...". But Ian's mother and her giant car and me, we all know that you can't tell anybody anything. You can't warn them. All alarms are false.

When something this bad happens, you look at whoever is standing there, and it seems like they are welded to you. There isn't any walking away. When we picked up our son's ashes, Brad let me stay in the car at the crematorium, parked under a giant magnolia tree; that thing had to be about a hundred years old. The other crematorium, the one where I had to go to pick up Granny's remains, was a brick, professional-looking outfit with a room full of vessel options. I casted about in terror for over half an hour, looking at chunks of marble and granite that all looked like "Salesman of the Year" awards. The plaques said ridiculous things. One had an excerpt from "Thanatopsis." I started to giggle, then I started to sob. The crematorium officiant—is there a word for such a profession? Something compact and dignified? The cremator-in-chief thought I was having a mild breakdown and brought me a glass of water. "She hates... Bryant... so much," I choked out, between sips. Finally he directed me to a discreet wooden cube. It was beautiful. I flew all the way back to Seattle with it in my lap. Before 9/11 and all those x-rays.

We chatted a little on the plane, but I was just teasing her. She was not there. "You're traveling now, old lady. I hope you set your hair just right. It's gonna be a long ride."

This crematorium, however, looked like somebody's house. Somebody's granny's house. I started sobbing then, thinking about my Granny. She didn't have a house. What if she'd had a house like this? What if she hadn't lived with us? She's dead. She never had a house, a whole one. I can't give her one now—that will never happen. Never. This case is closed. It's just a little room here. We can't stay.

Once I started hyperventilating, I got out of the car. It was Sunday afternoon, and nobody was anywhere. I mean nobody. I grabbed onto a low magnolia branch and started touching those dark leaves, how they look wet but they aren't, none of them were. I started touching all of them I could reach. I couldn't decide if I wanted to pull off the whole branch and destroy it, rip it to toothpicks, or if I wanted to pull myself along it like a rope and hug the trunk of the tree that had been here before my granny and all of us. That tree was more careful than anybody I knew. I looked at it and waited. I let go of the branch and got back in the car before anybody saw me acting that way.

I don't think we had any packaging options. It was a little white box, narrower than a shoe box. Like a box for an elegant table game, one played with stones, like Go or Pente. Something it took years to master and to which ancient medi-

tative texts had been devoted. But the outside was clean of
any instructions or any demonstrations for what your strategy
should look like. Like an entirely white Rubik's Cube. And
equally pointless.

I used to have a recurring nightmare in which my father
chased me while riding a piece of farm equipment. Sometimes I was riding my bike, and sometimes I was running—
sometimes I'd start out riding my bike and my bike would just
start disintegrating, like the dreams when my teeth fell out of
my mouth while I was talking. Chunks of it would fall through
my hands, sometimes turning into animals or tiny wheels or
anything that could run away from me when it hit the ground.
In the dream my father was always yelling the same thing over
the noise of the tractor motor and the clanking of the bush
hog trailing behind it: I'll erase you! I'll erase you!

I thought it was only a dream when I told Mom about it.
She says it really did happen, when I was about seven years
old. But she says he was yelling "I'll race you" when I was riding my bike home from the neighbor's house, that I was coming down the driveway and he was mowing the grass. She says I
just misunderstood the whole thing.

Sometimes in the dream I hear breathing closing in and a
thumping Edgar Allan Poe heartbeat that is probably my own
blood behind my eyes. Sometimes—but this was much later—
he would also be shooting at me.

The box was shaped like a minus sign. Deleted. Erased. It
was my job to write him back.

Granny, the world erased you a long time ago. Her name
was Hilda. She erased herself. She tried to burn herself
down, inside a little closet. If it had worked out for her, her

ashes would have been lost in a crime scene in Belleville, New Jersey, about seventy years back. There's too much damage, the firemen would have said. The fire started on the second floor. Looks like just one casualty.

Chapter Six

ALL THESE HOUSES. All these families inside them. Every new place means a conversation, but who are they? There's no online tutorial to speak that language.

I'm not sure whose bad idea it was to honeymoon in Charleston, South Carolina. But in the trajectory of my first marriage, it wasn't the first or last bad idea, so assigning blame requires a lot of imagination. And it's always less satisfying than you think it will be, anyway.

I held on until that one antique store where I passed out backing over the threshold while a tremendous breakfront china closet shouted obscenities at me. It wasn't even that old, a high Victorian piece, dark mahogany and ridiculously ornate. Angry, masculine but prissy, it was enraged about someone taking the silver. An art deco vanity on the sidewall just cried softly, the same way my grandmother's dresser used to. Women and mirrors. That's where it all goes sometimes. Come on, you've been creeped out by an old mirror before. If you'd just be quiet for a minute, most times you'll realize it's just all the sadness and disappointment.

Charleston's pretty old for a New World city. But not as old as Conza. I've been trying to get to Conza, Italy, where my ancestors lived, since my parents went there in the 1980s, after the big earthquake. But I'm going to need some kind of sedative or something, being that it's an active archaeological dig. I get enough stories from 1940s apartment houses and ugly furniture. Plus, all that shouting might be in Italian. Wait, no—not Italian. I don't know. Some ancient language— some untranslatable Samnite dialect. Then again, I don't really hear language when things happen. So it'll be like a test case. We'll see if I can even tell what's happening.

I'm getting some outside help on this trip now, which for years has been hypothetical only. But I've decided as soon as I can get this ash business settled, I'm going. I found Emiliano, an archaeologist from outside of Naples, on the internet, and he says he can help me locate any living family members I might still have near Conza. I have a whole collection of photos I found online of the earthquake's aftermath. That's where my grandparents' relatives ended up. Under a pile of upturned Samnite rubble.

The Samnites are non-Roman, savage, and fascinating. Evidently they practiced human sacrifice. Often a firstborn son. Bad harvest, bad weather. Bad omens. They were a rough, sallow race. "Non-Roman" understates their situation: they were Roman haters. They'd fight the Romans with anybody. Hannibal hung out in Conza while kicking Roman ass. And when the Samnites attacked the Neapolitans, the denizens of Naples went tattling to Roma. These baby killers again—would you please rid us of them? Conza was founded by the Irpinians, an even crazier Samnite subset, the people of the wolf. It happened like this: alongside infanticide in the Samnite toolbox, there was a kind of voluntary banishment that concealed itself in the heroic narrative of the Quest. Young Samnite warriors were invited to leave the tribe in search of spirits in the form of wild beasts who would lead them to new fertile lands, or possibly eat them. It would seem, then, that I descended from hardy-hided, abrasive, combative wolf-chasers who perched on top of a precarious, volcanic mountain until the earth, having bucked them for years, finally gobbled them down whole.

My mother went to Conza right after the earthquake. One of my father's relatives owned a gas station nearby, the only one for miles. Overcome with gratitude at the arrival of American kin, he closed the gas station and laid out a feast of folkloric proportions for his guests. My father seemed to be able to communicate in Italian only about the subjects of food and profanity (a true Samnite—anger and the belly), so dinner probably progressed with little trouble. My mother ended up talking to the local priest, who came over as word spread in the community about the visitors. He agreed to take them up to Conza itself, what was left of it, after they were fully fed.

Passing the accumulated line of cars at the gas station, the priest drove my parents up the brick roads, straight up the broken mountain. "Look," he told my mother, gesturing at a life-size lion statue lying on its side next to the road. "All kinds of things like that one. The earth just opened up, and out it all came. That lion is older than Christ."

At the top, they got out, but the priest warned them not to go far. Archaeologists hadn't shown up yet. They hadn't been able to remove all of the bodies, but anyone who was still missing... well, anyway, that's the only way they could count the dead. Who was still missing. Sides of houses had slipped off like curtains falling. The breakfast dishes still on a Formica table, the cereal box still standing. Bottles in neat rows on the shelf. The kitchen towel across the stovetop. An apron on the back of the wooden chair.

I told my mother that Emiliano would find anyone who was still left. "You need to," she said. "There was another cousin who was in Naples, I think they said. You need to find him. I don't know if the gas station is still there."

"If he stayed, he's a rich man now. They rebuilt a new Conza five miles down the road."

"There was another cousin," she said. Then she looked away. "They're mostly dead, you know. You know the rest of them are dead."

Emiliano said he could find the records. And he was an archaeologist, and about the only way to go to Conza is with an archaeologist. It's an active dig. Plus, there's still sinkholes and all. And the earth knows it hasn't swallowed every last Samnite yet.

I left Francis a message about the knocking. He'll know what to do, I'm sure, just like he knew what to do about the Santeria spell. I don't know, but I'm betting this ritual's going to be a little more complicated.

"Hey, Francis. Sorry I keep missing you. I'm calling... well, I'm wondering... I have a question for you about All Hallows, and I had some knocking, I mean I heard knocking. On the front door, you know, at midnight. I kind of, I had been doing a lot of thinking this year, but didn't make an altar or anything, I just... well, I got really caught up in Edgar's robot costume and I have been kind of trying to move away from this dark stuff anyway, but the knocking was pretty pronounced and it was too spaced out to be acorns, and by spaced out I don't mean, you know, 'weird,' I mean 'at regular intervals,' like four times. Five times, maybe five times. Listen, this got to be a long, awkward message. I need your help, maybe. I think. Should I just maybe pour the water on the steps again? How would that be? Probably not in the same arena, I guess. Well, it can't hurt—or can it? Oh shit. Let me know something. When you get a chance. No big rush. I'm good here. I burned some sage. I loved your Halloween pictures. I miss Halloween with you. I miss you. Call me back."

Okay. Okay. I should have mentioned the dreams. But I doubt it would have made much difference. Time to think about something else.

Dear Emiliano:

Your fee seems quite reasonable, and I would like to proceed. It looks like the date is set for next October. And yes, I would like very much for you to do what you can to locate my relatives, even the dead ones. Especially since there might be more of them. I would like to know, as closely as possible, where they lived in the town. I know it won't look exactly like it did when they were there, but I'd just like to see the sky from that part of the mountain. After all these years, I bet whatever was left of their houses has been blown into the valley or taken away by archaeologists or goats or wolves or something. I have groundhogs in my yard and they get into my trash. It's either them or I've got some raccoons. Invisible raccoons. Do you have raccoons in Italy? If not, I'll see if I can bring you some.

I am making some pretty good progress with Rosetta Stone. I'll at least be able to talk about men, women, and children who are eating or reading. I really hope I get to some more complicated concepts before I arrive next year, like "What was the name of the family that lived in this house?," "Where was the location of the church before the earth's crust broke it open—east of here? West?," and "How many days after the earthquake did you find the last survivors?" I don't know the Italian term for "phobia"—I will be sure to look it up before I get there. Rosetta Stone's not giving me any traction at all on concepts like "What was your unfinished business with the living?," "Are you in trouble now for all the ritual sacrifice?," or "What's it like over there? Dark? Cold? Is it like a Frank Stanford poem? Is it like a Chopin nocturne? Are you still even listening to us out here? What about peace—did you find it? Is that even what you wanted? Have you ever ridden in a dogsled in a field of stars and snow?" Because I hope it's like that.

CHAPTER SEVEN

WHEN I MEET THEM, THE GHOSTS, it's not always the age of the place that matters. It's not always the grimness of the circumstances. It doesn't have to be something especially creepy or brutal or horror movie-ish. One of the longest stories I ever found turned up in a New York brownstone of a friend, decorating for a Christmas party. I don't know exactly what they want, but it's probably simple. Like I said before, sometimes they just want you to feel. The truth is, I like these two. They've got chemistry. Or should I say electricity? They've got a connection.

I felt everything about them, all at once. The only way you can feel it is for me to tell you their story, as much as I know it to be.

Smoking ruined Vivian's coloring, along with her once-celebrated singing voice. She can't always remember the lyrics—but she can always make them up.

"Mata Hari wore a string of pearls

To cover up her lovely girls

But when she danced they all had fits

'Cause when they swayed, you'd see her—"

"Vivian! Please."

George only pretends to be sensitive. He's much younger than Vivian. Maybe thirty?

"Georgie, you don't like my song? I'm wounded."

"Just... I'm... I can't fix the sink when you're—"

"Okay, okay. You want an artichoke?"

"I don't see how that could possibly help right now."

"I mean when you're done, Mr. Smartass. I got currants."

"I'd say yes, but I feel like I'm about to be the brunt of another punch line."

"That's no way to go through life, Georgie. You need to loosen up."

"What the hell did you put down this drain, Vivian?"

"Feldstein's cat. That sonofabitch."

"Well, that explains the hair. What did you say you dropped in here?"

"It's a pin."

"Why were you washing a pen in the sink?"

"Not an ink pen. A brooch. I got some peanut butter on it and I was rinsing it off."

George stuck his head out long enough to give Vivian a dramatically baleful glance.

"I was making seed balls for Harry. I got the peanut butter stuck in the filigree and I—" Harry the parakeet squawked in his cage, as if to back up Vivian's story.

"I think I see now. How big is it?"

"...about the size of Feldstein's pecker."

"Viv!"

"It's about an inch, inch and a half—little amethyst in the middle. I won it."

"Okay. Let me guess. You beat out Dorothy Parker for the best recipe using arsenic as a garnish."

"I won a spelling bee."

"A spelling bee?"

"Don't be surprised, Mister. I was a good student, a good girl. I won a scholarship, too. They took that away. But I got to keep the brooch. Heh."

She'd turned away, wiping down the kitchen counter in slow circles—like a bartender, George thought. He came all the way out from below the sink, a handful of goo from the trap in his rubber glove. He wasn't bad at this plumbing thing. Maybe this would be a better career, more stable. All morning, he'd been nursing a vision of himself with big muscular arms, rolling up his sleeves and carrying a toolbox into peoples' apartments, saying things like "Don't worry—we'll have your tub drain working again by this afternoon," and collecting the gratitude and generous payment from friendly housewives who'd offer him cold beers or Coca-Colas—

"They said a girl didn't need to go to college, so they gave it to a boy."

"They gave your scholarship to somebody else? Who gave it away?"

"The school. It was a college in the mountains—they offered the scholarship to the valedictorian of the school. That was me. But the high school said no, you don't need it; you're just gonna get married and waste all that fancy knowledge."

George wasn't sure what to say. It didn't sound fair. Could she be lying? he wondered. People had always been unfair assholes. That was certain. And it always seemed like the bullies were taking away what belonged to the weak. Anything worth having, anyway. He thought of the high-school girl Vivian, before the cigarettes and the Final Net. He wanted to storm into the principal's office and say, What? Something loud. Something with sweeping gestures.

"Georgie! You saved the day again. Good boy."

He looked down and saw the flash of silver in the pile of rotten muck in his hand as Vivian's talon swooped in and plucked it out like a city pigeon grabbing your popcorn.

"I sure thought I'd never see this again. Thought it was pinned to a sewer fish, swimming out to sea."

"There's no such thing as sewer fish, Vivian."

"You don't know much, Georgie. You've never seen the inside of a sewer. The size of Volkswagons, those bastards. Oh, look there. Now it's back where it belongs."

All wiped clean, she had fastened the little silver bar to her blouse lapel.

"Gotta have something to leave behind for posteriors."

"I think I will have that artichoke."

What do you think? It's a pretty good story. She reminds me of my Granny. But maybe that's just how I tell it, that's how I keep the feeling from that day, like a piece of hair in a locket.

Keep your eyes open. I'm sending you my words, my maker, in white clouds of breath, no sound. Even when the wind stings them, keep you eyes open, or you won't ever know what happened. It's fading already, and it's cold here. Just keep your eyes open. Listen.

CHAPTER EIGHT

I'M WATCHING MY NORA out the back window, stalking something through the trees with her camera. I'm drinking coffee; her black trench coat patterns with red maple as she pushes the branches like turnstiles. It's after work and daylight savings has kicked in, so we're short on time with these leaves and what they've got going on in this good light. The gray is creeping up on me right now while once again I sit here with the dreaded crock of Granny in front of me. I've been tasked with giving it up. I watch it for a while, moving the coffee pot that sits on top of it. Changing her Tennyson book out for her Longfellow.

> *"Come, little leaves,"*
> *Said the wind one day,*
> *"Come over the meadows*
> *With me, and play;*
> *Put on your dresses*
> *Of red and gold;*
> *Summer is gone,*
> *And the days grow cold."*

She got me to memorize that one from a notebook. It didn't have a name. One fine day during my work on Columbia Granger World of Poetry, a CD-ROM project providing snippet analyses of the most-anthologized works of poetry in English, I found out it was George Cooper who wrote it, not Granny. I'd already found out to my disappointment that she wasn't actually Longfellow or Ella Wheeler Wilcox or Felicia Dorothea Heymans, so it wasn't a big shock.

I don't recognize our yard in Nora's pictures, tiny universes of insect domiciles, intricate webbing, arterial leaf patterns. Twigs. Or roots. Or entrails, I don't know—some kind of gray, frayed tubes twisted around each other like an elaborate wrought iron gate. My favorite photo of Edgar is one she took; she's so close to him you can see the capillaries in his cheeks, a reflection that looks like artificial lenses in his gray blue eyes. He's looking up. You'd have to be invisible to get that close to him so unguarded. You'd have to be a ghost bubble, a floating orb, breathing against his blue veins, the family trait. I used to be embarrassed about my own obvious blue veins across my collarbones and chest until one day somebody admired them. I said I'd always tried to hide them as much as possible, sometimes covering them up with Dermablend, the scar- and tattoo-obliterating stuff they use in the movies and photographs. He protested. "That shit is what we are made of. Don't cover that up."

The vanity of all that covering, looking back, kind of baffles me. I never tried to hide my actual scars, even the ones on my cheek and neck from when my grandmother's dog tried to chew my face off. Deano, her devil-Chow. That was a truly pissed-off dog. I was four years old, it was a hot summer day, and I tried to blow on his face because I thought it would cool him off. He was solid black all over, even his eyes, solid black balls rolling around in his boxy head. I'm still not sure why, but Granny held me up to the mirror after he bit me so I could see my broken face. "Look what you did!" she yelled at me—but she was far away, it seemed like, and the only thing I could see in the mirror was the white thing my teeth were sitting in. My jawbone. My skull.

Back then, my mother took me every three months to a portrait studio downtown to have my picture made. You can see in those photos lying side by side in the brown leather album a parade of frilly panties and smocked dresses, ridiculous child-sized purses and wide-brimmed satin-trimmed hats, then hair longer and straighter, combed carefully and clipped to one side, a crocheted poncho, a tiny necklace with a single pearl. Then finally a brown jumper, glasses, and a massive red tear from the edge of my mouth along the jawline... My pediatrician recommended some minor plastic surgery to get rid of the last of the scarring. My parents fought about it over dinner that night. "It's not like that's the only thing between her and Miss America!" my dad said, scooping up his cucumbers and vinegar. He ate a big bowl of cucumbers and vinegar almost every night. He thought they'd make him live forever.

I've loved the tiny smile that lived on my face next to my mouth for my whole life. Over the years, it's moved a little and a little more, and now it rests right at my jawline. But it's still there.

What I remember of that day of the dog attack, in Granny's bathroom, is all in pieces: her screaming and my bones out there in the open, smells of metal and Adorn hairspray. She saved every ancient perfume box, ones her husband had given her in the forties and fifties, lined up on a rickety étagère barely hanging onto the wall. Shalimar and Chanel No. 5, turned sour years ago. Creams. Boxes of soaps. Boxes of hairpins and hairnets. A giant metal box of buttons. One time she held a knife to my face in that same bathroom. I can't remember why. I just remember the cold air around the blade. I was on the toilet and she wouldn't let me get up, held the kitchen knife so close to my mouth I could smell the metal and feel the cold. She was shaking, angry.

She's in my box now.

She's not nice. She was never nice. But she was there,

and now she is supposed to be gone. But whatever she was, I still have it. I'm supposed to be deciding what to do with it. Nobody else wants it. No one cares what I do with it. Got any ideas? She hated the outdoors. She hated the South. She disliked most people and mistrusted animals, despised them for depending on her. "Everybody wants you to do something," she told me one time, late in her life, in her last apartment where I tried to get her to talk to her neighbor. Well, at least to answer the door for the woman. She liked dirty jokes, moustaches, and England, but only because she'd never been. She liked Muhammed Ali and Henry Kissinger. She liked books.

"Scatter them someplace she liked. Have a ceremony. You need to let this woman go," says my therapist.

I did exactly what she wanted for her funeral: had her cremated, refused all flowers, and played Dean Martin singing "Please Don't Talk About Me When I'm Gone." Her one surviving sister hugged me tight. I'm pretty sure the only place that old broad would want to be left for the rest of eternity would be inside her own mind, with Longfellow and Whittier and of course Mr. George Cooper.

"Dancing and flying
The little leaves went;
Winter had called them
And they were content—
Soon fast asleep
In their earthy beds,
The snow laid a soft mantle
Over their heads."

She did like snow. What am I supposed to do with that?

If I can shed the same tears for the same reason a Nineteenth century woman did just because I sat down at the same dining room table, why can't I know what Granny would want me to do with her ashes? Good question. So far, it hasn't worked that way. But I'm not sure I'm giving it my all, really.

I work hard at lots of things. I make a lot of lists. I don't make those "bucket" lists, though. First of all, it's morbid. Second of all, I wrote a movie script that some troll at a now-defunct big studio puked all over, calling it "a meditation on deliberate living, or some such nonsense." The troll particularly ridiculed a subplot involving one character's "Life list" made for a fourth-grade project, then kept in a time capsule. As the story goes, this guy believes he'll be sent to prison for planning a fake bank robbery and stealing peoples' pets, so his friends attempt to help him complete the items somehow before that happens. Not only did the studio reject my script, pieces of it showed up a few years later in that simplistic atrocity everybody in the world seems to have seen. If you're going to steal art, make it better or something. "Bucket" is an ugly fucking word.

But anyway, before I die…

I tell Thomas routinely that I would die happy (one day, much later) if I could ever, one night, in a crappy coffee shop or wine bar, sing in front of people without traumatic incident—traumatic for either me or for the audience.

"I'd give up every bit of writing ability I may or may not have if I could sing. Even just for a brief moment."

This train of conversation always kind of pisses him off.

"You could sing. If you wanted to. I've told you over and over: all there is to singing is being fucking fearless. You've got to own it. You've got to not give a shit what anybody thinks of you. You can't be afraid."

I repeat, but only loud enough for me to hear, and only after Thomas has gone outside: "I'd give up every bit of not giving a shit what people think of how I sound on paper to not give a shit about what people think of how I sound out loud."

Sometimes even talking is hard. Asking, though. Asking is pretty major.

⚡

They were so close, so close, so close. The in and out of their breathing started to be comforting—it came and went with his heartbeat. They could eat him any time they wanted. That was fine. He didn't care about it anymore. All he knew was the last breath and the next, in out, in out. Moving so fast through the dark and the cold.

CHAPTER NINE

IT OUGHT TO BE an okay conversation to have with your therapist: how to disposition the human remains you have accumulated. Don't you think that's reasonable? Wait. I'll rephrase that here in a minute.

"I have two sets of human remains in my charge, for which I am solely responsible. Pretty much. And that's been true for a while, but I've only been thinking about it lately. I bet this happens all the time."

Wouldn't you venture that therapists hear that kind of thing a lot? Turns out not really. I guess most people get embalmed and the going-in-the-ground part is a given. Does everybody have funeral plots? Because my friends don't chat about this kind of thing. Okay, so who do people talk to about this stuff? It makes Thomas uncomfortable, and my mother is far too cavalier. I don't think she takes it seriously at all. When Granny died, my mom told me that my grandmother had asked to purchase a funeral plot at Montlawn, our town's massive, commercial, nondenominational cemetery. Maybe there was a sale, because Mom picked up a few plots. She likes a deal.

The last time she was over, we stood around the kitchen counter mapping this out, because I wasn't buying it entirely.

"I find the whole request to purchase a burial plot strange, since Granny daily threatened to come back and haunt me if we put her in the ground." I can see about how this conversation might have gone, and I expected I wasn't getting the straight story from Mom.

"Well, she has one," Mom said. "And her mother and father are buried there..."

"Granny tried to stab her mother in the throat with a cake knife."

"...and your father has one there..."

"Her son, who threw her out of the house she had lived in for thirty years. On Mother's Day."

"...and I have one..."

Here's where the whole thing started to get suspect, so I questioned her a little further. "Let me get something straight: you have a plot with Dad at Montlawn?"

"Well, Joel's is there, too..."

"Joel's plot? So, you, and your two husbands... and Granny's parents... This is sounding less and less like a party she would want to go to. Anyway, she wants to be cremated, so that's it."

Mom looked like she had more on her mind. "Shit-eatin' possum"—that's the name she has for this facial expression.

"You've got a few more plots with a few more names on them you've purchased, don't you?"

"Mmmhmm." She had opened up a jar of Mt. Olive Sweet Midgets and was crunching away. You may not have Mt. Olive Sweet Midgets where you are. I know you can't get them on the West Coast, because mom used to bubble wrap three or four jars at a time and send them to me in Seattle. I got my friends hooked on them, and then I used them like money.

"Well, you can take my name off that guest list. I'm not going in the ground. By the way, are you planning to be flanked by your husbands like backup dancers? Or are you going to have yourself divided and distributed?"

Mom scanned me disapprovingly. "Don't you even own a proper pickle fork? I can't get in the jar right with this one."

The last house Granny's parents ever lived in was the first place I ever knew was haunted. Those stories were sad, dull-edged, blue-shadowed. The people in there felt like crumbled up papers.

The house was across the road from the house I grew up in. I used to walk over to visit my great-grandparents, Little Granny, as we called her, in the kitchen frying up pieces of cornmeal for the dogs. She'd give me a bowl with butter and bread. Sometimes a warm apple fritter wrapped in a cloth.

"Go on in the living room," she'd say, and I'd go see Great-Grandaddy. He had pockets full of butterscotch disks in crinkly orange cellophane.

"Who's that?" I'd ask him. "That man up there on the stairs."

Great-Grandaddy would lean up in his chair close to my face, blocking my view of the stairs, my view of the man's black lace-up shoes tapping on the landing. "Don't you pay him no mind," he'd say. "Don't mind him. He ain't studyin' us."

That woman out back of their house, though, near the cookhouse and the shed—she was old. She didn't make a sound. She was always looking for something she used to take care of. Maybe chickens? She moved in little circles, little figure eights. I felt her worry while I dug holes to bury old Coca-Cola bottles with notes inside them.

My therapist asks me if I have my own funeral plot. I tell her she should probably ask my mother, because somebody put her in charge of the seating chart for this event. Little does my mother know I have found a place that will turn your

departed loved one into a firework. I've never been more certain about anything in my life. I think I'll have them choreo-
graph the display to Leslie Gore's "Sunshine, Lollipops and
Rainbows."

I hadn't ever really contemplated the long-term implica-
tions of hosting someone's remains. I guess you've put that
together by now. Here are some new points to consider,
if you yourself are either in this situation or find yourself
confronting it in the future: So what if something happens to
me? Do people bequeath other people's ashes to their heirs?
There's a nice parting gift.

In my case, it won't matter. She didn't like anybody else, so
I couldn't do that to her or to my heirs. She was really proud
of this cocktail napkin she had from the maiden voyage of the
Queen Mary, so I briefly thought about taking her out on a
transatlantic cruise and dumping her halfway between New
York and England, the two places she had the warmest feelings toward. But if an angry spirit comes and asks you what
the hell you meant by dropping her off in the middle of the
ocean... I mean, it's not like you can go back and fix it.

Granny hired a nanny for my father when he was a baby—a
handsome woman, a retired sharpshooter, an Annie Oakley-
type from a real Wild West show. It's a funny thing to say,
but it was true. That Hilda, my Granny, she really didn't like
anyone. She set herself on fire. At least once.

I like a mausoleum in theory. But I've read a lot of Poe,
and so that plan seems fraught.

It shouldn't be like the little wallet of relics, the Saints'
bones—one of the only things I have that belonged to Granny's husband. He died of cancer when my dad was a kid.
They're not mementos. I found his grave, with his parents,

in a big Catholic cemetery in New Jersey. She can't be buried there because she wasn't really Catholic. You can't take pictures, either, and you can't visit unless you're family. His parents, Concetta and Nicola, didn't speak English. They didn't want them to marry any more than Granny's Southern family wanted her to marry an Italian. I have the letters the lovers wrote while Granny was waiting to move to New York so they could get married—

Dear Tony, can't I come now? My aunt has cursed me and said she hopes I fall on the church steps and break my leg on the day I marry you. Has your mother gotten out of bed yet? Will she learn to like me? I've stopped working at the restaurant but Daddy says I can't stay at the house any longer than May and I will have to find someplace to live…

Dearest Hilda, my life! I can't tell you how excited I am that you will be coming soon! It's not so long now. If you can just wait a few more months Mama will come around. I know she will. She is already softening to the idea and she knows I will not have anyone but you.

They never accepted her. When he died, she left New York with her little boy and what she could carry. She thought the Italians would kill her son. Concetta and Nicola were buried with their boy Fiore, the little flower. And only the family can visit. Hilda is dead. By the time my dad lost our house to the bank for the last time, no one was even talking to him anymore, and we lost track of him. So there's no family left for them. Those graves. They're lost.

CHAPTER TEN

EVERYWHERE YOU GO, there's some dead piece of somebody that won't stay down. You may not know it's there, but it is. It's in the air like electricity. It won't just reach out and shock you most days, but let's say you scuff your slippers along the old carpet a little too vigorously one fall morning, and...

Nobody argues about that presence, where I come from. What they do argue about is barbecue. It's a game that's as pointless as fistfighting over whose mother's red sauce tastes the best. Nobody remembers that the answer is always where you were born, and that's the only answer. It tastes better because memory tastes better than anything.

But Sam Sampson's Barbecue waits there on the corner for the wrecking ball, and it's pissing me off. I don't even like Sampson's as much as some; in the barbecue debate, I've always sided with Walker's, a nondescript cinderblock outfit in Franklin County. Nora and I are standing on the corner across from Sampson's. The building's empty these days, now that the restaurant moved to a new location down the street. Not everybody moved, though.

"When you're born empathetic, if you can't find some people you like to listen to, you start feeling sorry for plates of peas," Nora points out, staring into the crosswalk. She is used to seeing me like this. I've missed a couple of opportunities to cross the street. The new restaurant that's here next to us, it keeps turning for me back into the old Heilig-Levine furniture store where my uncle Arthur used to work. We got our scratchy green couch there, and my grandmother's coffee table that used to be our coffee table. It had ovals on it like brooches. I used to try to pull them off so I could wear them.

I take the ovals, the coffee table, the green couch and Uncle Arthur and kick them down into the storm drain with my boot. We've got to cross the street on the next turn. He wasn't really a blood relative. We called them aunt and uncle because they helped out my father when he was in high school. This storm drain is dark—and it's deep.

It was a tearful toddler moment when Nora begged me not to make the food talk to her. Food items, dropped and forgotten dirty gloves on the sidewalk, a piece of fabric from outgrown pajamas, decrepit buildings. They all spoke to her, asked her for forgiveness. She doesn't ask why we haven't crossed the street yet. In a minute, she'll take my hand.

When she does, I'm still thinking about having to walk past Sampson's. Because when that building goes, a little more of downtown gets erased, and we'll put something else there, and I want to stop letting people like me off the hook for throwing things out and starting over. It's like we drove this brand-new car that is our whole civilization off the lot this afternoon, and immediately it lost half its value. I'll tell you my story about Sampson's, as much as I can explain.

Let's say, though, that one afternoon I decided not to eat the sandwich I had brought for my lunch at the office. Let's say the other stenographers had said "Let's go down to Sampson's and get some barbecue," and I had remembered how much I liked their Brunswick stew, and then checked my purse to make sure I had the three or four dollars it would take with still enough to stop by the pharmacy for Mother on the way home.

All I know about this one is that I am her voice. This is how it happens. I usually don't know who they are. They want the story told, sometimes. They're lonely, and sometimes they don't seem to know what happened or where they are. She was alone and afraid, everything changed. It's like she died there, but that's not where she died. But she did stop living, and I can't tell you if she ever started again. That was why she was still there, a piece of her left unaware of the whole rest of her life, whatever it may have been. I don't know her name.

I heard her that last time I picked up lunch at Sampson's for the office. Waiting in line, I think I saw her face there for a second in the Coca-Cola mirror, this shocked look, perfect lips. Not like girls today. You can tell when they're from another time. I've said all along, I know who's there and who's not. I'm not crazy.

She was scared, maybe because I could see her. But I'm never certain if they know I can see them or not. Please don't let me see you, I think as hard as I can, and I think they know if they want to talk to me, they shouldn't scare me. The man behind me in line, back in the real world, he touched my elbow for a second. He didn't see a thing except my white face and my panic.

"You need a hand?" He pulled out a pressed handkerchief. He had nice little round glasses like my friend the lawyer from UNC. I think they're in a secret society, the round glasses men.

"Whew! Just got the vapors there for a second. Must be allergies."

"My hay fever started right up this week. Gonna be an early spring. Say, let me get you some water..."

But she was already walking through my skin, leaving the jolt of her pain up and down the map of my veins. I wheeled around the restaurant, but I didn't see her again. That's because by then she had told me everything—

The other stenographer and I locked our desks and walked
the four blocks to Sampson's, said thank you to the old man
in a boater hat with a red-and-blue band who held the door
open for the young ladies so the bells just jingled a little bit
on our way into the lunch crowd, the steam from the kitchen,
the clear, sharp smell of vinegar and the musty undercurrent
of smoke and pork, the black-and-white pictures of men in
more hats in black frames scattered over the walls, the music
of the orders called back to the cooks in beats that sounded
like pieces of words chopped into bites, and then let's say that
before I could smile at the counter man, I saw in the next-
to-last booth against the far wall my fiancé—the accountant
I had met in line at the Department of Motor Vehicles three
years ago when I got my first driver's license, when I had to
leave college midway through my second year when Daddy
died, and this young man spoke to the officer at the counter:
"Now see here, she has her paperwork and has passed the test,
and you could show her some respect—there are plenty of safe
women drivers, it's 1962 after all, not the dark ages," and
then bought me a cup of coffee after—if in Sampson's that day
I had seen my fiancé, my great savior on whom I had come to
depend for advice and consolation, in the next-to-last booth
on the far wall, with the secretary from his office, heads bent
close, hands—oh, his hands covering hers, laughter flutter-
ing over the dull chimes of silverware to plate, forkfuls of
steaming pork moving in arcs into the talking mouths of all of
Raleigh, all of those people knowing, all of them looking up
suddenly, like my fiancé, suddenly looking away because I was
a stranger to them—they never accepted me here—

Everywhere you go, there's some dead piece of somebody,
the electricity running alongside us like a third rail. Let's say
I would swing the ball myself into Sam Sampson's. I'd swing

it and swing it. I'd leave nothing but dust. If that would fix it. If that would minus her out of existence. If it would take her pain back to a place for the things that never have been. I liked her. I wanted her to exist. But not like this.

Decisions like these really shouldn't be left to one person. I know an awful lot about history and people, all about cultural taboos and stuff like that, and even so, I don't have the qualifications I'd want somebody to have, say, if some kind of feeling was all that was left of me on this earth, being bounced around. I'd haunt, too, is all I'm saying. But I'd pick somebody better. There must be somebody better for this job. But they keep on finding me. They keep telling me. Not just the girl at Samson's. What about the brakeman on the train in the mountains who never said anything and kept turning away, just a husk in a great black raincoat. And the little girl laughing in the hall outside my old office in the school basement— "Aw, she just wants to play," the old night watchman said when I told him about her.

I checked the message Francis left again:

"Sweetheart. I'm going to need a few more details. Don't panic."

It was a good meditation phrase, the message. I got to thinking about it. Best written in a circular fashion, because it works in any order. I always like writing repeated-phrase verse forms—sestinas, ghazals, rondels, anything with refrain. Heck, if you've got a couplet, you're halfway to a villanelle. Somebody told me that one time.

I've got a flawless plan when human reason fails.
Sweetheart. Don't panic. I'm going to need a few more details.

See, that first line will be totally ironic by the third stanza.

But I'm really sick of irony. I can't take it seriously anymore. I seriously cannot take it anymore.

Sweetheart, don't panic. I'm going to need a few more details.
Message received: the world is off its rails.

That's an overstatement. I am completely, entirely, fatally over overstatement.

Within about a decade, three poets used this elliptical form to write about death. I know—a poem about death, how freaking unusual. But all three of these had this kind of strain against the creaky, wobbly end of life—a desire for something sweeping and operatic over the small rooms and whispers—Dylan Thomas, of course, the one everybody knows. William Empson's "Missing Dates" and Roethke's "The Waking" don't say it as loudly, but both mark the fear of slow decay, the partial fires, the waste that remains and kills. The poems lost. The missing dates. All my villanelles got silly. I wrote one about a creepy librarian at Duke, stalking people in the Gothic Room. I wrote one called Godzillanelle. I couldn't rage, rage against the dying of the light so I kicked it until it was dead.

Great Nature has another thing to do to you and me. Francis, it's not just the knock at the door. What do I do with these people and their heartbreak? And what about the two broken hearts I need to hear from? How do I clear the line for them?

I'm going to need a few more details. Don't panic, sweetheart.
I'll hold your hand, because life is love, and don't you know that love is art?

CHAPTER ELEVEN

WHAT CHAPS MY HIDE MOST about the Doomsday preppers—even more than the colossal waste of money and human
energy on the scale of mountain climbing and scrapbooking—is their sense of entitlement. Their behavior displays
an enormous sense of self-importance, as though the future
of human existence swings on the fulcrum of their personal
survival. Every other sane person in the world works every day
to keep from being sucked into some kind of shithole. But
the Doomsday preppers spend all their time looking for new
and various shitholes to pray to and for. They've made a re-
ligion out of themselves and their own lives—what can they be
thinking except that natural death has already set them aside
as the chosen people? It's like they asked for invisibility and
a bulletproof carcass in their letters to Santa last year. Here's
the news, though: I can see you, you dung beetles. And you're
going to cut your fucking hand on an MRE in your fucking
underground aluminum tube and die of gangrene, slowly.
You'll get cancer. Or you'll just have a heart attack.

But these mundane demises—the Doomsday prepper has
already dismissed the possibility of such ignominy. For him,
Death is a defeatable opponent, not the cloaked skeleton with
a sickle, but a masked luchador with a nuclear explosion on
its chest or a dollar sign on its forehead. Or, a zombie.

On a related note, I'd like to point out that the current
fascination with zombies is a total analogue to the 1950s
fear of aliens and swamp creatures. It's good old cultural
xenophobia, the secure-the-border mentality of a bunch of
yahoos looking through the dining room drapes at the new
neighbors across the street. I'm nobody to judge—I think

there's going to be an apocalyptical invasion, but it's going to be big fat unhealthy people riding their hoverrounds in every possible public place. We'll have to leap over them in the grocery store, the mall, public restrooms, church, community interest meetings, dance recitals, sporting events. It'll get hard to vote, eventually, because it'll take two fucking days to get through the line. There won't be handicapped parking anymore, but regular parking will be well outside of town.

It's my issue, and I'm working through it. But if you're hating on the zombies, I suggest you practice some self-reflection. What is it you really fear—the undead? Or terrorists? Who's taking our jobs, you wonder? Foreign accents? Democrats? Or is it the produce in the grocery store that you can identify neither as fruit nor vegetable? How long do you cook this? Do you have to cook it? Do you add sugar or salt? What language is that? Does anybody buy this stuff?

In the shopping cart, Edgar holds his hand up to his ear like it's a telephone. He's facing me, but his eyes are looking far left. Nora is resisting asking. His lips stretch straight across, appraising. Once in a while, he glances over at us. Rolling through the bakery, he points at the free cookies and raises an eyebrow. Nora grabs two, hands him one and takes a bite out of the other. Edgar smiles and nods, starts to chew on his thoughtfully.

"Okay," Nora says. "What's Edgar doing?"

"Looks like he's taking a rather serious phone call."

We're skipping the alcohol aisle. There's this big logjam of thirtysomething-year-old women in front of the box wine, probably because Hoobastank's "The Reason" is playing on the store sound system. It's a wall of static anxiety, the pointiest static of all. I can almost hear one of them sobbing. She's

got on wedges that are about a half size too big and a Liz
Claiborne skirt. She's a clerical... no, she's a paralegal. It
sucks, too. She had this thing with her boss, and it broke up
her engagement. She's too proud to go back. Her mother—
no, her grandmother thinks she's engaged to the lawyer, but
he's already married, and her dementia makes it too hard to
get her to understand... Then who was the boy at Christmas?
How will I pay for law school now? Why won't he leave his
wife?

"That's just weird," Nora says. She has seen me lingering
in enough public spaces to know when I'm tuned into somebody's narrative. She looks at me, over to the paralegal, then
back at me with a brief raise of an eyebrow.

"You're so darn cuddly," she says, mussing Edgar's hair in
short, awkward sweeps.

"You were a sharp little thing at that age yourself."

She squints at him. "But then, the things he says..."

"No weirder than your Poodle Planet," I say.

"What? Oh. That. I don't remember any of that. But from
what you told me, that all made perfect sense."

"Oh sure. Aliens bringing emotions to earth in electrical
form... why not? On the other hand, he watches us transmit
an entire array of human feeling every single day into a tiny
chunk of glass and metal."

Nora is still watching him. With the hand he's not using
as a communication device, he picks up a box of crackers and
shakes it. She shrugs. "You're right. He's probably broken."

"I don't know. All of us would be, I guess—I mean, we all
saw people talking on telephones before we knew what they

were." I'm just testing this theory. It's turning out to be a grim one.

"Yeah, but the old ones at least had wires and stuff. They at least looked like they were connected to something, like there was something on the other end maybe. Now we're just talking to a box. Not even a box. A... tile."

Edgar has been shushing us. He just shushed a young woman who was speculating with her bearded companion as to whether the chicken they were selecting was free-range. Previously, by the bananas, he shushed an old woman who had called him a little cutie. I envy his ability to shush people with impunity. I can't seem to escape their burdens in the grocery store. It's like everybody comes here to ponder the sorry states of their existences. Every brand of beer reminds someone of an abusive uncle. Every bag of cat food is a lost childhood pet. By the time we reach the dairy section, I'm exhausted.

"Nora. Nora. Nora." An interruption on the cereal aisle. We were stopped, because the chocolate Carnation Instant Breakfast was on the top shelf and about three boxes deep, because nobody but nobody ever buys the vanilla; it only serves to confuse and block access to the chocolate Carnation Instant Breakfast. Confounding this central principal of grocery physics, I was utilizing a box of vanilla Carnation Instant Breakfast to dislodge a box of chocolate and coax it close enough for me to fetch it down. Instead, it just slid completely off the shelf and landed with a muted slap in the cart itself.

"That works. Nora, your brother needs to speak with you."

"Miss Beverly needs to speak with you."

"What?"

"Miss Beverlyyyyy..."

On rare occasions, Edgar's imaginary friend Miss Beverly sent a message to one or another of us. It was pretty unusual, though, for her to ask to speak directly.

"I don't want to talk to her."

"She wants to talk to you."

"No." Nora shook her head and held her hand up in surrender. "No, I really do not want to speak with Miss Beverly. YOU speak with Miss Beverly."

"No no no she says Nora I want to speak to Nora!"

"No! I can't talk to dead people!"

We joked about Miss Beverly's spiritual provenance all the time, but even as it came out, the whole "dead" thing landed with a much more resonant thud than the box of Carnation. Edgar's eyes got big, and he straightened up in the cart.

"She did NOT DIE."

"Okay, okay. I'm sorry. Please tell Miss Beverly I'm sorry. That was a mistake."

"She did not die. She did not."

"Okay, Edgar, we got it," I said. "Miss Beverly is fine."

"She did NOT die. She did not DIE."

This conversation careered thus through the soft drinks. The ability of the human mind to block out the odd and unusual never fails me. The necessary level of focus to locate something both diet and caffeine-free seemed to be occupying the consciousness of everyone in our vicinity.

"Edgar, Nora has apologized to Miss Beverly. Is Miss Beverly upset with us?"

"No."

"Okay. That's great. Does she need to know anything else from us, or are we good?"

"We good."

"Excellent news. Let's move on."

But in the frozen foods, one last quiet time, Edgar whispered in my ear as I was bending past him, "She did not die," almost making me drop the bag of peas.

I could sweep together the dust of our hearts. The ashes of my grandparents' house that didn't burn. The complete fire that is death. The charred wood and the pulverized concrete and the souls of a million barbecued pigs. The dust in the corners of basements. Everything that isn't the fire itself, the movement through the wires. Everything in the way of getting through. All of it rolled up together and shot into the sky, into a firework—that's a song you could sing out over the radio. The ones on the other side can hear us, then. If we can roll all of it together and name it out loud, send it out into space on transmitters or something—then they could hear us. If they can hear us, then we'd be able to hear them, too. That makes sense, doesn't it?

If I know I'm in my final days, I think what I'll do is make myself a map of the recent installations of home fallout shelters and bunkers. I'll pick up a clipboard and rent myself a white sedan that looks a lot like a government vehicle. Heck, if it's my final days, I'll steal an actual government vehicle. And I'm going to drive down the twisty driveway of every doomsday prepper I can find, and when they answer the door, I'm going to say this: "Good afternoon, sir. Everything you have believed is correct, and the time has now come. The New World Order is upon us. Because of your proactive, forward thinking, my committee has listed you on the pro-tected rolls, and we wish to notify you that the alien invasion, financial collapse, zombie apocalypse, terrorist attack and/or chemical assault is imminent. Please take this cell phone into your facility, and we'll give you a call when it's safe to come out."

"Jesus. Why is the ice cream aisle so packed? Make a deci-sion. Everyone knows you're either chocolate or vanilla. Just know what you are and be it. Staring at the cartons won't change a thing." Nora returns with a half-gallon of Breyers and takes possession of the cart.

And once they shut the door on that sucker—the preppers, the betrayers of art and community—I'm going to take the bricks and mortar out of my trunk and go full-on Montresor on them. I'm going to seal them right on in with their six months of supplies. It's the least I can do. Maybe I will dedi-cate a song to them on the radio. Maybe they will hear it down there in the ground.

Nora has stopped in front of the eggs, staring at the rows and rows of large, extra large, jumbo ovals. Her eyes fix on something else, though.

"What if all of them are broken? What happens when they grow up all broken like that?" She turns her face to me. "What if we broke them? Talking into tiles? What will they break?"

Meanwhile, I'm stopping myself from asking Edgar who he's dialing up there on the hand-phone. Stopping myself from asking my son to make some calls on my behalf. He doesn't even know what's happening to him. I'm supposed to be helping him, not the other way around.

I want to take back what I said about scrapbooking, which was a harsh and unfair judgment. It costs very little, it does result in a made thing, and somebody might look back at that thing one day and feel a little jolt of happiness. But still, fuck mountain climbing. Sideways.

Chapter Twelve

I FOUND OUT MY FIRST SON WAS DYING while I was pregnant with him, so I tried to get to know him as much as was feasible. His heart only had two chambers. He could have had a heart transplant when he was born as long as there wasn't other organ damage—but there was.

"This issue is genetic," my OB/GYN told me over the phone one afternoon. "You will likely never be able to have children. Come to the emergency room now so that we can perform a C-section." He was pretty impatient with me, like this whole thing resulted from some paperwork I had filled out inadequately. At one point, he suggested that I had inflicted some damage due to overconsumption of water. Eight glasses a day was entirely too much, he said.

But when I woke up in the hospital, there was a nice young doctor I'd never seen before instead of the fat, balding, self-important jackass from the suburban Raleigh practice who had told me over the phone that I was too stupid to have children.

"We could do a C-section, and this could all be over," the new doctor said, "but if you think you can handle it, let's have you stay pregnant as long as possible." Six months earlier, as I sat at the kitchen table staring at a pregnancy test with three of my grad school friends, the words "this could all be over" might have sounded better.

I had never wanted kids in the first place. I wanted to live alone. I wanted to travel the world and write and be above all this crap. But this doctor, who seemed smart and sad and serious about something bigger than just my situation, stood there beside my hospital bed, waiting for an answer while I sized him up as just another person I'd met in the last six months who seemed to have business with me. Like I got handed the wheel of the car unexpectedly.

I used to have that dream when I was a kid, over and over, that I was driving the car too young, unable to see over the dashboard of my mom's Cadillacs and Lincolns, weaving all over the country roads. It was always nighttime in the dream, and usually my whole family—Mom, Dad, and Granny—would be in the back seat, fighting and smoking. Sometimes there would be other voices back there with them, people I didn't even know. I'd be pulling the wheel with my whole weight to one side, thinking I was coming up on the big curve in the road just before the Presbyterian church on the way to the grocery store. I couldn't see where I was—I'd just figure I was at the curve. I'd try to ask the people in the backseat but they couldn't stop fighting long enough to answer. Then I'd get scared they weren't even back there, that I was just hearing their voices on the car radio. And then I'd end up the field sometimes, rolling and spinning.

Dr. McMahon waited for me. Even though I knew it wasn't possible, it almost seemed like he had already spoken to my son, had some kind of conversation resulting in greater understanding on all sides. That's weird, I know, but that's how it seemed. "Do you think you can? If you want to do something for this child, this would be it. This is your chance."

I did want to do something, yes. It was kind of a sorry choice, but it was something, and I was glad to be doing something that seemed better than pointless. Six months ago I wouldn't have done this for anybody. So I guess I must have gotten to know him a little already by then.

There were a lot of tests. One was an elaborate variation on amniocentesis, and I had not one but two anesthesiologists, handsome ones, attractively placed on either side of my head for the procedure. It went on all afternoon and seemed like something that ought to be measured with a calendar and not a clock. One of them looked like George Clooney. The other one pointed out the resemblance to me when they first arrived, as if to get that out of the way.

"He's not George Clooney. That throws people off sometimes."

"Oh. Well, as long as I don't end up in a coma, I don't care who you aren't, really."

They watched the ultrasound screen with me, probably to distract me from the item too large to be called a needle.

The non-George Clooney kept me talking. He leaned and squinted at the image on the screen. "So that's the head—oh, I see it now. Yeah, you are better at reading these. At this point you've probably seen more sonograms than we have."

I told them how to find the heart. You could see it, the way it was really only half of one. Beating frantically. Trying to keep up.

"Wow. Oh, yeah. I see it. His hands—those are his hands? He's got them up around his face just like a boxer."

I felt pretty awake; in fact, everything seemed very clear.

"You know," I told them. "This building has a lot of stories."

"Oh yeah, it's huge. They're building an even bigger one across from the parking deck." The one who wasn't not-George Clooney nodded and smiled. He was more of a Steve McQueen type.

"No—I mean, people die here. Stories."

"That's... that's certainly true. Hey, how's about checking that gauge? Dial down, yeah. Okay. You're okay. You might be getting a little too much, but you're good. Keep talking."

"People die, and you know, they aren't finished. You can't just wipe that away—"

"Let's keep your hands still, remember. Gotta keep really still."

"Oh yeah. I forgot. I mean, especially the ones that connect them to their people. The things they did together. What they said, and what they meant to say. The stories. They get stuck here sometimes. You can't see them or hear them. Well, sometimes you can."

"Well, nobody's going to die today. We're on this."

"You're pretty." They laughed, relieved to see the horizon again. But I wasn't done. "You're pretty, but you can't say that. Nobody can say that."

I shut my eyes for a minute. But they made me say the alphabet backwards, and for a little while I forgot everything that was happening.

For two more months, I talked to my son. His heart stopped beating while I was in labor, but I got to see his face finally, after the delivery, after the intensive care nurse sat in the dark with me for an hour and only said one sentence: With all that go wrong in this bad world, it's a wonder anybody ever get born. He had a dimple square in the middle of his chin, like Kirk Douglas. I come from a family rife with dimples, but not in the middle of the chin. I touched it. I thought, this is the worst moment of my life. It might be the worst moment of my entire life, not just so far. Because it's awful enough that I can't figure out where to put my eyes or my brain. I looked at everything in the hospital room, the bed sheets, the IV bag, the needle taped into my arm—I stared at that, at my blood, wondering how I could live past this. That room became a capsule of reality, and everything, every other existence outside, quit existing while I held my son. I no longer believed in a world outside the capsule. I would have to learn to believe in all of it, all over again.

As a modern memento mori, the intensive care staff takes Polaroid pictures of the babies that don't make it. They put it in an envelope so you can look at it if you feel like it later. In about a month I took it out. Wrong baby. I kept the picture anyway. I hope his parents did the same, and in a little way, somebody else out there knows our sons, at least a little bit.

I moved west right after, drove a van full of books from Raleigh to Seattle, like a pioneer. I even faced off with a buffalo. A single, average-sized buffalo is bigger than a minivan. If there were more buffalo just around, we might have a better sense of scale as an entire culture. I tooted my little minivan horn at him, and that fucker shook his shaggy head at me, like it tickled the inside of his ear—in all that woolly mass, I could tell eyes, ears—what a creepy train wreck of an animal. I couldn't believe in such a thing until it rammed my vehicle. I locked the minivan doors, and then I thought to myself, What the hell good is that going to do. I'm a piece of limp bacon in a little lunchbox. But he's not going to reach over and open the door. He might roll this minivan off this hill, scattering me and my books across a national park and making for some kind of darkly humorous USA Today headline: "Reading Not Fundamental for Bison." "Buffalo vs. Bookmobile in Desert Deathmatch." "Librarian Gets an Overdue Lesson from Nature." "Mythic Creature Doesn't Believe in Minivans."

It was a pretty good trip. I saw a bunch of places I had only read about growing up, so it was one long collision with the Real, and not just bison. Took my picture at Calamity Jane's grave and sent it to Granny—that's what she always called me. I had a little problem in the Badlands, though. It was a top pick on my list of places to see, and I counted down the miles until we crossed the park border and then... I can't explain. I think it was my first panic attack. Except for the minivan itself, everything was so bleak and old and alien—I kept thinking we had been sucked into a time vacuum and a dinosaur was about to come bounding out at us. "Don't stop the car! Don't stop the car!" I started shrieking.

"Don't you want to get out and walk around?" Brad thought I was joking.

"For God's sake keep going! Don't slow down!"

By that time, I thought if we even rolled down a window, we'd fill the van with air from Mars, or whatever this planet might be. That our heads would explode and we'd die.

I finally calmed down when we got to a ranger station. But I had horror movie music playing loudly in my head by then, and it didn't stop all night. There's a photo of me, pay phone in the crook of my neck, arms wrapped around my waist. I made Brad stop at the ranger station so I could call my mom, because I was certain I would not get out of the Badlands alive. It abhorred people, that place. We had reserved one of the tiny cabins in the middle of the park to spend the night. I pulled down the blinds, turned on every light in the cabin and slept with a heavy flashlight in my hand, fully dressed un-der the army blanket on the bed. I waited for it to come and get me, that thing in the park. I swore the next morning that the rocks were all in different places.

In the light of the cabin, I kept seeing floaters like before a migraine, but around the windows and the framed maps on the walls. The air hung thick and prickly, full of static. It was hard to breathe, and the long cries outside didn't sound like an animal. At about 3 a.m., I got up and wrote. It was a sonnet, short one line—I lost it somewhere over the years, but it was about desire, about how no matter how long you live, even if it was forever, it's not enough. I felt like I was trying to get a drink of water out of an ice cold fountain that was at a tiny trickle, that I was swallowing it all down into an endless belly, and that the water was going to stop any second. That thing crying outside was cut off. It knew I was cut off, too. I crawled out of the Badlands the next day and swore I'd never come back without knowing a lot more than I did then.

Dr. McMahon stayed in touch with me until my daughter was born three years after all that. I flew back to see him when I found out I was pregnant; I knew he'd be the only one I'd trust to tell me she was going to be okay. He hugged me and gave me the name of a friend of his where I lived on the West Coast. I turned at the end of the hallway and he was still standing, watching. He waved me on and smiled. A year later, he was dead, too, of lymphoma.

What do they want? Are they running from me, or am I running from them? I'm flying but I'm sinking down into your fur, beasts. I'm going to be one of you. Will you let me?

CHAPTER THIRTEEN

"WE COME HERE KNOWING THINGS. When we're little babies. And you have to tell somebody, before you start to get big and forget."

The Seattle Metro bus is late. It's already wet everywhere, and the benches are soaked. I'm hoping it'll get here before the next round of rain. Nora is four years old.

"In the house, the food is in the kitchen. We eat the food in the kitchen, and the food makes us grow up. We ride the bus to the store to get the food. The buses run on electricity. And the electricity is, the electricity is in the wires up there, see, where the bus touches it with its magic wand. So it goes. It's in the wires but it's also, also up there in the air. The electricity is everywhere. They brought it here."

The number 5 bus is now really late, and I'm holding Nora's hand tight because yesterday a taxicab jumped this same curb and hit a homeless man who was just standing here. Phil and I were standing in the doorway to the bookstore when it happened. These taxis come flying off the viaduct, nobody's paying attention, and...

"They brought it here a long, long time ago from outer space."

Nora tells the best stories. Sometimes she'll say This one is a poem, so write it down, and so I will. She's been spinning this one for a while, and it seems to have acquired a different kind of momentum. She's getting more theoretical in her fourth year. I'm scanning for the number 5, but I'm pretty riveted to find out how she's going to bring this whole electricity-from-outer-space concept back around. I try to leave the lulls, not ask any questions. You get a lot more that way, and there's more integrity to the sense of it all. I want to know: how did they get it here? Who are they? Where'd they go?

But like most humans, I don't know which questions are the really important ones.

"A long time ago, they came here from their planet with the electricity in their bodies. Before they came here, there weren't any people, because we needed the electricity, you know, because that's how bodies talk to each other. We couldn't be here before that."

Oh, man. Where were we then? I need to take some notes.

"But when they brought the electricity, the bodies jumped up! Because then we could see each other and talk to each other. And it was so great! We wondered where we had been for so long, and we talked and talked. Because then, we could love each other, and before that, it hadn't been. And we were so excited! So everybody started dancing around with the electricity. And it made us all find each other! Because we could see! We could see each other then, and we were all over the place."

Her voice keeps gaining force and expression as she narrates. I pretend I'm looking up for the 5, but I'm staring down First Avenue remembering that beautiful poet from Kashmir who I met at a writers' conference I went to years ago, before Nora was even born. I could see him dancing toward me in his celestial robes, drawing his forcefields in the air with his limber hands. That insipid song, but still. As he drew near, he shouted over the music, "THIS! IT IS A WONDERFUL SONG!" It was not a wonderful song, not before. But I will never forget the gold threads of his garment in his shimmering retreat and re-approach. "IT IS ALL ABOUT LOVE!" he called, directly into my ear, brushing my cheek slightly with silk and a rush of air. A little electric shock—the same electric shock I felt reading a year later of his death. What a poem he gave me, one heart-filling moment in this world. I love this momentary vision. All this time, I still think about it, especially on the days when nothing is gold, nothing is electric.

"They brought it here to us, and then they went home. To the Poodle Planet."

"Pluto?"

Oh, no. Don't break the spell. Don't hear me and my adult voice of brittle fact.

"Nononono. Not Pluto. Pluto little Pluto is the farthest planet from our sun."

"And it's not the same?"

"No. It's not the same. The Poodle planet is the Poodle planet."

"Are there poodles?"

"What?"

"Are there poodles on the poodle planet?" Is there any way for me to explain the wrongness of my questions?

"Not poodles. Poodle Pla-net."

This case is closed, and I disappear again for a little while into the irretrievable world of Not Child. I lose my innocence again, like I do at least once a day every day since I became a parent, and someone hung each and every one of my internal organs outside my body, where the birds can bite at them and strangers can mock me.

Something feels wrong about taking a celebrity death personally, but I miss Lou Reed being in the world. I guess I'm kidding myself when I think something feels different without his energy here. I kept following the stories in the news, not really knowing what I was looking for (short of oh look, he's over here—this was all a terrible mistake and he's fine!) until I saw something his wife Laurie Anderson wrote about his death, and all I could think about was Lou Reed going back to the Poodle Planet with a heart full of love and wonder. "Dazzling," Laurie Anderson had said, having witnessed his death. Even in the pain, dazzling.

Laurie Anderson, I too believe that the purpose of death is the release of love. I'm really sure she is right about that part. All of it. I'm doing something wrong, though, and I'm going to have to figure out how to fix it. I can't ask four-year-old Nora. Teenaged Nora doesn't remember the cosmology she gave me. I'm going to have to figure it out myself.

Lou Reed got awfully screwed by this particular universe, early on. It's pretty great news though for all of us, if you think about it, that you can have this kind of turnaround. And I don't think it's just the universe making it right—you got electroshock therapy from your rotten parents and rotten doctors they hired to make you something more like the son they ordered out of a catalog, so here—we're going to give you the sweetest death scene anybody ever had that actually ends in dying and not spontaneous recovery.

I don't think it works like that. I don't have enough faith in fairness—truthfully, I'm pretty sure the scales are always tipped. I've always taught my kids never to say "It's not fair," the ugliest words in English alongside "I just don't think of you that way," and "last call."

No, I think Lou Reed came here from the Poodle planet with a bucket full of lightning. I think if you bring it, you get to take it with you. That's not hard to believe, is it? It's pretty much physics, right? And maybe if you don't bring enough, there's even a chance to make some.

What do you do with somebody who disrupts the current, though? Because one way or another, you have to take care of that.

There's a service available to prospective house buyers that will determine whether any deaths or heinous crimes have occurred at your potential address. I don't look into it, because I'd spend all my time checking out every house that ever looked at me sideways, and I don't have time for all that. I'd like having some circumstances to match to my knowledge. Some verbs for my nouns. At least in some cases. The ones I've really wondered about wouldn't get covered in this kind of investigation, though. Like the Mell Avenue house in Atlanta—when I moved in, I didn't realize the house itself had a reputation among local musicians. Some of them called it "Mama's" or "the Mama house." Split sometime in the seventies into multiple residences, it seemed to attract troubled people to it. But while living there, many of them would experience a clarity that had escaped their reach previously. Whether it was a bad relationship, drug problems, or general lack of direction in life, most people moved out better than they came in. It was the place where I decided not to be a smoker, out on the stoop with my pack of cigarettes at sunup, before my coffee even. My neighbor in the next duplex came out onto his stoop in his pajamas with his pack of cigarettes, and we crouched there like two awkward gargoyles. Don't be this, something said. Come inside and have that cup of coffee—it's cold outside. I sat on the couch in that living room

and wrote a letter to William Harmon at UNC. I'm watching
Bill Clinton's inauguration on TV, I wrote, and I'd really like
to come home now.

I came back to North Carolina three different times before
staying. I wouldn't have come back the last time if it weren't
for Nora, but I didn't want her to grow up with the two of us
floating around like orbs, unattached and hollow. The house
we moved into, divided into apartments like the Mell house,
was mostly quiet, except for a ball of electricity in a room we
decided not to use. It was so bad the TV wouldn't work in
there, so we just filled it up with stuffed animals. That seemed
to help. It's hard to scare people when you're buried under pink and purple plush. The place had a great, rambling
porch—that's where we met Thomas, so our times there were
all good. He plugged in our Halloween pumpkin—my mom
bought Nora this giant pumpkin, since she'd grown up living
in a tiny apartment in a big city, and Mom wanted her first
Halloween in North Carolina to be special, so she got this big
plastic piece of yard décor and dropped it off on my porch.
Nora was all excited about getting that sucker plugged in but
there was no outlet outside, and I was taking the whole thing
as a personal failure.

Then we pulled into the driveway just after dark, work,
school, commutes and groceries behind us. I was tired. And
Nora started to yelp.

"What? What on earth is it?"

"Pumpkin! Look at the pumpkin!"

"What about the—oh."

The giant grinning orange ball fixed its triangular gaze on
us from the porch, glowing like a champ. A white extension

cord ran along the floorboards of the porch, up the wall and into my downstairs neighbor's window. I had a little conversation with myself at this point: That big tall man downstairs has touched my pumpkin without so much as a by-your-leave, because he thinks I am some fragile woman who isn't strong or smart enough to plug in a pumpkin, and he's about to get a piece of my mind. I am providing an example of strong female self-sufficiency for my daughter.

"What does that mean?" Nora whispered. Meaning the pumpkin, though I suspected she could hear my thoughts. It's why I forget to tell her things.

"It means..." I said, thinking carefully about what the world looks like and what it acts like, and about being a little girl dreaming about driving a car full of adults. Thinking about people, about loving them, about electrical wires and transmissions. About fear, the fear that the little outline you leave in this world is made out of nothing but light, and you'll be the echo of a dream somebody had one day. "It means we're back in the South."

She turned to look at me, but got distracted by movement in the headlights.

"Oh! Oh! What is that? Is that a rabbit in the driveway? How'd that get here? Call 9-1-1! Don't we need to call 9-1-1?"

One day back when I lived in Atlanta, I came home from work to the Mell Avenue house, crawled under the covers and listened to King of America over and over for a day and a half. Every time "Indoor Fireworks" came on, I'd sob. "Sleep of the Just" would start it up again, too. Then I'd fall asleep for a little while. Over and over. You like people for a while, and then you hate what happens, because there's part of you

that knows if you were gone they'd get over it. It's unfor-
giveable. That crackling, searing loneliness, though. It just
pushes you back to more people. It's a dance, a dance to a
stupid song. The smart songs tell you what's going to happen if you keep on dancing like this, but you're going to keep
dancing, because the radio keeps on playing the stupid songs,
and you keep hearing the itchy sound of a transistor like bad
AM transmissions. Drown it out with poems and cigarettes.
But you're coming back. And you'll come back happy.

When I dream about the Mell Avenue house, it's the
dream I had about it before I ever saw it. The first thing I
noticed were the hydrangea bushes, high as the roof line,
hiding the screen porches on either side. Snow cones, I used
to say when I was a kid—somebody had them, an old house in
the country. But these were the biggest ones I had ever seen,
blue as a baby's eye. In my dream, I came through the front
door that had been nailed up when the house was divided into
apartments. Everything was dark, but then a slender blond
man, so pale he was like silver, came down a set of stairs, attic
stairs, and his arms were full of the hydrangeas. He smelled
like blackberries, his breath like he'd been chewing violets. I
woke up from the dream disappointed and confused, trying
to attach him to something, and then I forgot the dream until
a few years later, living there, when I dreamed about coming in through the front door again. I went over to the other
side of the house and found it, the old threshold, there in the
floorboards. You could even see the worn pattern of all the
ins and outs. I just never noticed before. Once every year or
so, I dream about the house still, but always from the street,
outside the hydrangea bushes. And I never saw the man again,
but in the dream, I'm always looking for him. He is always
waiting for me.

I miss him, the silver man. I don't think he's here in this world. I miss him, but it's not like the keening voice in the Badlands, the one that made me want to hurt myself and still wakes me up. The tattered voice, the rags of a dead woman's desire, the angry ravening being who wants back what was taken. In the poem she made me write, I said This world's time will never be enough. She hates it here, the desert. I don't know if she's dead or what, but she can't get out, and she hates us all for going on without her. But the one who trapped her and then left her there—she hates him most of all.

The frozen air hits my lungs, and it feels like a shriek, but I can't hear my own voice. Nothing is coming out. No sound but the breath of the beasts. I think they are wolves. I think they have already caught me. I think that's why they don't get any closer. Where are you? Are you a wolf now? Where are we?

Chapter Fourteen

You know how living people will tell you who they are pretty soon after you meet them? Dead people do that same thing. They'll put it right in your path. And they are much less likely to be duplicitous—if they're trying to get your attention, they're not trying to trick you. At least I hope that's true. Let's keep that case closed.

The fact that what you know to be true always seems as normal as can be—knowing is the important part. Not imagining or even processing, because knowing is a lot faster—that part probably made me less likely to bring up any of this stuff or admit anything was going on. I mean, you see a cat, and you think about cat things. You think fur, you think claws, you think meow. Next you might bring memories of your cat from childhood, you might think of the Cheshire Cat or the Cat in the Hat, or you might think Holy Shit get away before I start sneezing—but all of that is next-phase thinking, it's all reaction. The first things are just the recognizing of catness and the feeling catness gives you. The reality of Cat.

It's the same thing with these historical transmissions. I'm going to call them "historical transmissions," not because I'm afraid you'll freak out or not believe me. I'm just trying to make it easier to name. First, you apprehend it.

It's as instant as sight, but sometimes it's broken up, like the picture flickers, the signal gets interrupted. You may not see, smell, taste, hear, or touch it (although sometimes you do). But you get the great physical sense of catness, or whatever it is, just as instantly as if you saw a cat. It's there, really there. It kind of messes with you when you try to prove it to yourself, though. Have you ever walked into a house and thought "I smell cake—somebody has made cake"? And your mouth waters for cake, you look at the empty cake stand but you keep hoping until long after you're out the door that somebody is going to offer you a slice. You survey your host for flecks of flour. You sniff again and again, and maybe you can still smell it and maybe not, but you start to convince yourself that it was just you, that you wanted cake so badly that you manifested cake smell out of your brain.

What is stranger: that the universe holds onto energy, and that some people see it sometimes when it gets really frantic or serious, or that we're all such incredible vortices of loss and desire that we hallucinate missing parts of our psyche on a regular basis? I'm not being flip; it's a serious question. One or the other is happening. Maybe both.

As long as it's not something that scares me, this knowing—seeing—this business doesn't really have much effect on my behavior. There have probably been some cases where it made me treat people a little differently than I might have otherwise, but I always thought of that as a hastening of the inevitable. The most obvious emanations from living people are duality, burden, and hazard. On that last one, I'm often not sure if they are in danger themselves or if they are the hazard. I give those folks a lot of personal space. Dual people have two levels of energy: the one that's talking and this other one— I get freaked out and don't like those people, even though that second level often has nothing to do with me, it turns out. But I really don't like being worked. I take it personally, regardless. People with burdens wear you out. They're worn out. Stuff is around them, and about half the time they don't even know it. History weighs them down. They are haunted.

(There's actually one other obvious emanation people have. It's the most obvious one, really. But it's kinda rare.

There are people so open to love they are messianic. They open your heart and scoop it out like they have a big invisible trowel. They can save you, but they can kill you, too, because a lot of the time they don't have any idea what they are doing. That's a completely different case.)

Unused as I am to activities without any sort of certification process, I've spent most of my life then having the occasional "note to self" moment or spontaneous conversation with an energy: "Whatever you are, get out before I see you and this goes badly for both of us." Thomas is a scientific mind, though. A fearless scientific mind. You show him catness and he will prove the entirety of Cat from the inside out. He knows me pretty well, too. The last time we visited his parents, we got up early and went down to the Donut Dinette. He had an idea.

"I want you to see this place. I'm not going to tell you anything. Just see what you get."

He drove me out of town a way I'd never been, out to the Uwharrie Forest. These mountains here are East Coast creatures, old and smallish, worn terrain, blunted and sloping. The car veered up the switchbacks, through the trees still thick with summer leaves. I kept trying to do that whole aligning-your-chakra thing—I'd been listening to a meditation podcast to learn how to do it. Nothing outside of modern dance classes has ever made me feel more like a jackass. At least both make your posture better. We're also talking, me and Thomas, about the demise of small Southern towns. Every time we come to Albemarle, I say "We could live here..." and he says "No, you could live here. I already did."

"Yeah. With all the empty storefronts downtown, I bet the rent would be relatively cheap. I guess home health care is huge here, with all the old people and the kids moving to the cities... Okay, not to be weird, but I want to go ahead and say that ever since we started up this ridge, I feel like there are men on the ground to the right of the car. Up that ravine over there. They're not quite crawling, but crouching. Were there Civil War battles here?"

Thomas knows a lot of the local history, and since I've got no idea where we're headed or what he's got in mind, I'm following his directions to talk about everything I see or feel. But he doesn't seem to know about the crouching people.

"I have no idea. There could have been. That's not why I brought you, but let's remember that. We can check it out later."

I keep going. "A bunch of men moving around. They might not be fighting. They're crouching, though. Moving in phalanxes, kind of. This would have been a long time, long time ago... There's another—there's a guy. Dark hair. He's not with them, though. He's hiding up here. He's doing something else. Maybe a thief or a moonshiner, but he's... going where he can't be found. Is this weird? I'd think I was making it up, except—it's different when I make up a story, when I'm making choices. This, this is like reading a magazine article, but over somebody's shoulder. Or while I'm half-asleep. I can't quite make it out straight, but I'm not making it up. There's parts to it, pieces. Maybe not all the pieces, but enough to know it's not mine."

"Do you know how a capacitor works?" For a second, I think Thomas has just gotten bored with my rambling.

"What?"

"Probably not—I'm asking because I think you'll like this. Give me a second."

"Okay."

"It'd be better with a diagram, but since I'm driving, just give me a second to get this explanation out."

"Sure, sure."

"Because what I want to get to is Poisson's Equation..."

"Like 'fish?'"

"What?"

"Poisson? That's French for 'fish.'"

"P, o, i."

"Two esses?"

"Yeah."

"Then it means 'fish.'"

"Well, in this case, it's this dude's name. If it's fish, too, then it's fish. So let me get the whole thing out, will you? And we'll come back to the fish part. Anyway, when you have a capacitor, the two plates—there are these two thin metal plates, separated by space, by air. You put a positive voltage to one side—"

"And a negative to the other?"

"Actually, usually just a ground—that's because voltage is all relative, all potential. We're getting into theory here though, and I want to get to this word I think you'll like..."

"Oh! Well, let's get there."

"Okay. So now the plates don't allow the current to pass from one side to another, in a capacitor. The electrons all build up on the voltage side, in a kind of slope shape. Because they've stuck there, they can't pass through, but nature—"

"Nature's got to balance."

"Always. So Poisson's Equation—that's what characterizes a semiconductor."

"Semiconductor. That always makes me think of a short man leading an orchestra."

"No, no—stay with me here. Semiconductors are the basis of all modern communication. Cellphones, microprocessors—semiconductors. Some assholes will come up with 'Meh, what about fiber optics?' And you answer them, well, dipstick, what's driving the fiber optics? That's right—LEDs. Semiconductors. We can't communicate without them."

"Well, maybe in some more traditional ways."

"Hang on. Almost to the good part. The working part of a semiconductor is the PN junction. Do not picture a train, please. Okay, picture one, but picture two linked cars made of dissimilar ionized materials. Before we get into some kind of advanced engineering course, I'm just going to say that the main thing you need to know with a PN junction is that, unlike a capacitor, a PN junction blocks the movement from one direction—but not the other. The electrons move from one side to the other through the PN junction. And that's modern electronics right there."

Thomas was the only engineer I ever knew who made electronics sound kind of poetic.

"Okay, so back to Mr. Fish. Mr. Fish's Equation is controlled by three main parameters, and these parameters determine the movement of the electrons. The first is electric potential, and that's what you've got available to work with. If you don't have enough potential to get things started, you can't get to the next steps."

"But if you got struck by lightning, say—"

"That would be too much electricity to be useful. Then you're just going to blow out—let's not derail, though, I'm almost there. Charge density—that's the electrons you've got waiting to move. The part you're going to like is the last—the moving itself, the action of the electrons moving in a unified direction when the potential is applied—the likelihood of that crossing over is determined by the permittivity."

"What? Like permeable?"

"No, more like 'permission.' And there's two T's—permittivity."

"Oh, that's so not a word. That is so delightfully not a word." Nothing makes me happier than strangers in English. Words I never expected to be there because I didn't need them before. I got distracted for a second because I was thinking about ways to use "permittivity."

"Just remember: LEDs. They make light."

"Oh! Yes. Yes they do. LEDs. Light bulbs."

Up the ridge, there was a dead end into a small parking lot. Thomas stopped and we got out. Outside the car I could really feel the dark man, almost see his face. He was out of breath and sad.

We walked up a set of wooden stairs set into the hillside. "Don't read any of the plaques yet," Thomas said. "I told you before about this doctor's house. Do you remember? I just want to see what you get here. Just walk around the buildings before you read anything."

Before he could finish, I could feel her, because sometimes I don't get to decide. She stood under the scuppernong grape arbor beside a little greenhouse. She was oriented away from us, but her being turned our way as I walked toward her. She had a little cat, and it was curling around the stakes of the arbor. She was aware of it, monitoring its movements. She noticed us for a little bit, but she was missing someone else, and it was like that was all she had to tell us. She had a cohort, but now she was alone up there.

The whole time we walked the doctor's property, she was the only one really there. There was another energy, from a woman, but not complete—it was just her rage and hysteria, rolling around up on top of that mountain. Like a chunk of that banshee in the desert, in the Badlands. It felt really bad. The other woman tried to keep me out of it—I went straight to this piece of land in the backyard that turned out to be the location of her garden, but I didn't know that then. It just said "Safety." But the howl of this other woman—like a cough, like vomiting—the back corner of the yard was full of that.

"You're not coming down?"

"No. No, I don't like this path."

"Come on—it's not as steep when you get past—"

I got two steps and my knees buckled.

"Nope. No. She's asking me why I want to go down there."

"Which one? The woman from the arbor?"

"I think so. She thinks this is bad for me. She says no. I'm going over here for a while."

So I ended up at the one-time garden plot, and this is where you get to say oooh, because I didn't go down the cemetery path. Something unnecessary was down there. Maybe just unnecessary for me. But I really couldn't walk down there.

A man on a white horse, coming up through the woods on the other side of the property. He might have been from a time before the house, though. He seemed unconnected. Coming through those woods on a horse—he'd come from the water, and he was mapping or something. Checking out the land.

And my lady under the arbor—one of the doctor's daughters. Missing her sister, who had died first. Sister? Yes. Sister.

"It's weird. I thought you'd get all kinds of stuff from the outbuilding where all the amputations happened during the doctor's surgeries. But you kinda cruised right by it."

"She doesn't like it over there. Her cat goes up under that house and it upsets her. He gets blood on his paws. That other guy is still here, too. He's really upset, and he's been up here a long time, still hiding."

"Maybe we can find an article—I bet moonshiners hid in the hills on Morrow Mountain."

"Well, sure. But that guy's there, and I don't need anything more to tell me. I only wish I had told him something useful. I just said, 'Dude, I know you're out here.' That's pretty lousy, when you think about it. I'm sure he's out there in a crevice thinking, Great. Thanks. Could you send better help? Because you suck at this."

I read the plaques before we left. Both of the daughters were sent to school in Raleigh for a couple of years. Later I found out they wrote letters home. The ones to them from their parents are in the North Carolina Collection at the UNC library—all written in schoolhouse French. And UNC has some of the girls' personal papers. The sister I saw was the plain one, the homebody. A gardener, she kept lists of fruit seeds, herbs, rose varieties. The younger sister—she copied Parisian styles into her St. Mary's School notebooks. She wanted to go places. Ultimately, she did, I guess. But not this other one. She's here on Morrow Mountain for the long haul, like she lost a bet or something.

Chapter Fifteen

It's not like a magic trick. I know all about magic tricks. I accidentally learned magic as a child from a professional illusionist named Vaughn, who must have made a bad deal at a crossroads. He'd become entangled with my father and was paying off a debt by teaching him card tricks. Vaughn was as close to Houdini as anything I'd ever seen in the far reaches of rural Wake County.

The whole enterprise of Dad and his magic lessons would have been vulgar and depressing—except that I was pretty sure I had willed the whole thing into happening. My devotion to Harry Houdini began with stories from Granny and blossomed with a young person's biography ordered from the Weekly Reader, which vastly expanded upon the tiny amount gleaned from the entry in my Childcraft encyclopedia. Dad was learning how to do card tricks, close magic, manipulation and distraction. He wasn't all that interested in the magic part—just the skill with cards. Vaughn and I were better than that, I thought, than Dad's gin tour of the eastern piedmont, the clandestine card matches of Kinston, Goldsboro and Dunn.

On Tuesday nights at six, Vaughn would show up early for my dad's lesson. Part of Vaughn's payment (or punishment) was the dinner my mom would cook for him. My mom had a short repertoire of Seventies meals: pork chops and pear salad, rigatoni and meatballs, hamburgers, hot dogs flayed and adorned with bacon and melted cheese, veal and peppers, country-style steak, and something she called "gwumpies," a kind of stuffed cabbage operation Granny had picked up from a Hungarian neighbor and passed along.

We were having gwumpies that night. That's what my mother called them, but I'm sure the term I heard her say is some kind of a squishy approximation of another word I'll maybe never locate. Like some of my dad's profanity, either Yiddish or Italian, or a misapprehension of either. Neighborhood murmurs. The smell of the browning ground pork and veal hung over us while we sat at the kitchen bar. Vaughn also came early to talk to me, or so I thought.

I watched Dad practice a Faro shuffle for hours every day for a month. I watched him because he made me—he didn't like practicing in a mirror, so he made me watch him and look for little things.

"Where was my right hand? Did you watch my right hand?"

"It was on the table. You picked it up for a second—"

"No, not this time. I told you to watch. You've got to pay attention."

Once in a while, he'd smack the table really hard, right in front of me, or reach over with a great sweep, stopping just short of slapping my cheek. Sometimes I was supposed to count.

"How many?"

"Forty-seven."

"Forty-seven, *marrone*, are you kidding me? You're counting fast. Say 'Mississippi' in between."

"I'm saying Mississippi."

"You're not saying shit. You're too fast. Do it again. Do it right. Dumb Dora's daughter."

I don't think Vaughn really liked my dad. I say that partly because whenever he'd teach me a really good trick or I solved a puzzle, he'd say things under his breath like Let your dad get a load of that one or Ask your dad that one—see how long it takes him to figure it out. A few times I told him some of the story puzzles, but he wouldn't even try, and when I told him the answer, he'd just say how stupid it was.

How stupid is it, I would think to myself, to engage yourself in congress with the dark arts so that you can take money from men in Bass Weejuns in the back rooms of low-end country clubs?

One night Vaughn brought me a little stick, green on one side, yellow on the other. When he showed it to me at first, he held it out in his right hand, turning it over one way and then the other.

"See this bar? You see, two sides? What color? See here... and now here... and now back here... yes? What color is the bar?"

"It's yellow."

"This side, and this side, and this side, and this side—a bar has two sides, usually. Two sides to an argument. Takes two to tango. Two faces of Janus. You know who Janus is?"

"It's the God who looks at the past and the future."

"That's right. That's right. This bar—see here, and see here—this bar is the staff of Janus. Two sides, top, bottom, top, bottom, what color?"

"It's yellow."

"And what does yellow represent?"

"Uhhhmmm... yellow roses are for jealousy..."

"That's a sad Victorian notion. Think bigger. Broader themes."

"The... sun?"

"That's better, yes! The sun—to which we all turn our faces, this side, now this side, yellow, yellow and OH! What's that? GREEN!"

"Whoa!"

The staff of Janus grew another side, evidently—a green one, out of nowhere.

"Green! The yellow has brought forth the green! But where has it gone? Is it on the top? Is it on the bottom?"

"It was spring, but now it's winter—the green is gone."

"Very good! Yes, the green is gone. Where did it go?"

I watched Vaughn's hand, the tips of his fingers where they rested on the edges of the bar. The movements slow, fluid, deliberate. Except I knew there was something fast, too, though—something I didn't see, because I wasn't supposed to see it. I was supposed to hear the story, notice his cufflinks, look for colors, not movement. Vaughn, like Houdini, acquired over many years a familiarity with human musculature and anatomy in order to create a base for his effects. They weren't illusions, entirely. He really could do things physically that other people couldn't do. And with the story—with the words, Vaughn connected up the whole world to his trick, to you and to him. A swirl of electrons around the nucleus of the physical, the movement itself, the thing. The rabbit in the hat. Your card. The staff of Janus.

"Put your thumb right there. Firm—don't let it slip. Now, the index finger is the one you are going to flex. The last joint. And then the thumb. It's two separate motions, but it's imperative that you treat them as one. Both must be invisible. You cannot react—you can't show the concentration in your face. You must be relaxed. You're just turning over a stick, see. You're only looking at the color, just like your audience. You're only thinking what color is it? Oh, there it is. Now. That's it, that's all it is. You just have to do it. A million times."

I carried the bar around with me everywhere inside my pocket, twisting it left and right, top and bottom. What color is it? What color is it? Watching The Jeffersons and Chico and the Man. It's yellow, yellow, yellow. Tentative on the inside (but friendly and calm without), I showed it to Rodney, a neighbor kid.

"This small stick is the Staff of Janus. What color is it?"

"Who's Janice? Give it here."

Rodney snatched the staff of Janus from me.

"It's yellow and green. What's the big deal? Crap, I thought this was gum."

I tried to sustain the narrative. "Watch! See, the sun is out, here, and here..."

"You don't have any gum?"

"Just watch—I'm trying to show you something."

"Like a magic trick? My cousin has a magic set. I can do the rings. You have to hit 'em in the right spot, that's all. It's pretty easy. I hit 'em too hard and they broke but they were kinda cheap anyway. Where are yours? Did you get the rings in your set?"

"I don't have a set. I'm trying to show you..."

"Oh. Well. It's just a stick, then?"

"It's the staff of Janus."

"It's pretty crummy. My cousins had a magic wand, and you could make this silver ball fly through the air with it."

It wasn't all like that, but I did learn from the first exchange to stand at least an arm's length away. And Vaughn showed me how to drop my shoulder, just a little. Makes people stand back, and they don't even realize it.

It was a tiny thing, but my staff of Janus made me feel slightly connected to Houdini. Like instead of practicing flipping a stick to baffle people for a few minutes, I might be perfecting the joint motions for hiding the tiny splinter of metal that I would later extract and use to pick the locks in which my handlers had enclosed my feet, my hands, my arms, legs, torso. The locks on the straitjacket I would have to escape in order to wiggle and winnow my way out of the trunk they had left me inside. On the bottom of a frozen lake.

Come back, I'd think, I need more lessons. Granny told me that Houdini's greatest trick, the one he planned all his life, was his return from the dead. He gave his wife specific instructions to follow. He was coming back from the other side so that we could all know what it was like over there. So we wouldn't have to be afraid. We could be free.

"Would you come back?"

"Where'm I going?"

"When you die. Will you come back and tell me you're okay?"

Granny mumbled something about being okay and being dead. She looked over at me, my giant scar along my jawbone.

"You don't need to think about things like dying, Nicky. I'm not going to die for a long time. I'm too mean."

"But aren't you scared of it? Isn't everybody? Couldn't you come back and let me know? If I died first, I'd come back and tell you."

"You're not no how, no way going to die. Don't you worry. Look at that cat—he's after my cardinal. Get away, you fat slob—I fed you fish; you don't need any poultry. That cat is a bastard. I wouldn't feed him, but he eats it when I put it out for the other ones, the shit."

So, this conversation goes back forty years. I told her I wanted to know. Maybe she's just trying to tell me. But what news is it? What's over there? If she's still staying here?

Where's the magic?

CHAPTER SIXTEEN

"WHAT DID YOU SEE? Tell me what you saw."

I was crying, and Granny had me by the shoulders, shaking me a little with each word of her question, the same over and over. What did I see?

"Nicky, you tell me! Tell me!"

What was it? I couldn't remember. Had I come in from outside? The door was open, a little snow settled on the red carpet, lightly, just like it flecked the grass out there. I must have been younger than eight, because the concrete patio wasn't there.

"Why did you go back across? You were all the way across the road. What did you go back for?"

The school bus had let me off. That's right. Why did I go back across the culvert? I was scared of the culvert.

"I..."

"Tell me!"

"I dropped something!"

"What?"

Why would I do something that scared me so much? It must have been important.

"A letter."

"A letter! A letter from who? That shitty Bess? Who'd you get a letter from? Was it from the mailbox?"

I had gone to the mailbox every day last summer, having one day, in a fit of boredom, written to "Chamber of Commerce" in the capitol city of all fifty states. For three months I got more mail than anybody in the house. By January I was still getting fliers with advice on planning my Miami Beach vacation.

"I don't remember! I'm sorry!"

She had let go of me and backed away, arms crossed, menthol cigarette ashes dribbling into her sweater sleeve. Behind the silvery cat's eye frames, tears rolled down her cheeks.

"I can't help you." That was all she said. She went out the back door and into her apartment, closing it up behind her, shaking the overdue Christmas pinecone cluster a little cockeyed.

I was watching Donahue when she came back in later and sat down on the couch. She almost never sat on our couch—I always went over to her apartment. She wasn't comfortable in my parents' living room. She dressed up and brought a purse on the rare Sundays or holidays when she came over and ate at the dining room table. We knew she came over to the house sometimes when we weren't there, but she never did anything except take things out of the trash. She hated for something that still looked useful to be thrown away. Remember those L'Eggs stocking containers, the big plastic eggs? I'd I come home and find the latest one back up there on my dresser like an accusation. Eventually I had to start breaking each one apart with a hammer before throwing it away.

She sat all the way back on the deep sofa, her legs so short that her little floral slippers floated just over the carpet, her feet not quite touching the floor. She didn't look at me.

"I saw a little girl in the woods one time. She was a beautiful little girl, with long hair in blonde ringlets. She was sitting on a tree stump, holding her knees."

She stopped there for a minute. She'd brought over her own ashtray and set it on the arm of the couch, and she fiddled with its beanbag bottom while she tidied up the end of her cigarette again.

"I said, 'Well, hey little girl, who's your daddy?' And she sat just as still as a rock. So I asked her again. I asked who her daddy was, and I asked her where she lived. Nothing. She wouldn't even look at me. So I got mad. I said, 'Be that way, then, you little witch!' Then she turned to look at me."

Granny got still, and her face drew down and darkened. "And I saw she was a witch. Her face was withered like an old prune. She had twigs and knots in her hair that had looked like ringlets. She hissed at me like a tomcat, and I ran all the way home."

She lit another cigarette before she got up. I didn't ask her anything, but she turned on her way out and, over her shoulder, said, "...and when I told Mama, she slapped my face and sent me to bed for lying."

Before she shut the back door, she looked at me one more time. "Better not tell them. Better not say."

I was thinking about that day. I could remember a letter in a looping alphabet, flowers in the margins. Was there a letter? A real one?

CHAPTER SEVENTEEN

"I RESCUED YOU." Edgar is perched on my shoulder, sort of, half-lying on me on the couch, half-propped against the arm. He's crawled up to put his face near mine to tell me this. His eyes hold onto mine.

"Yes. Thank you. Thank you for rescuing me."

Do you know how hard it is not to ask? But I don't ask.

I have a favorite picture of Granny. She's wearing a black dress that looks a bit Oleg Cassini via Ellisberg's in Cameron Village. It's probably about 1962, and she's in the foreground, leaning against a front porch post. Sitting behind her in a wide-bottomed, low back chair is a young man in a dinner jacket. His hair is perfectly groomed, and he smiles up at the back of her head while she faces the camera. She's closer but fuzzy; he's in sharp focus, but cut off just below his chest, in the bottom right of the photograph. They both hold their cigarettes upward, arms bent at the elbow, so that the jaunty tip of their little personal fires seem to close the whole scene in a set of tiny parentheses. She looks very Mrs. Robinson, before there was a Mrs. Robinson. I showed Mom the picture, but she didn't know much about the circumstances. Only some general information about Granny's dating habits.

"He rode a motorcycle, the last one. Your grandmother, she always had the young men around."

Mom always seemed both disapproving and in awe of her mother-in-law's behavior.

"That's not him. I don't even know who that is."

I don't know who it is. I know he looks like a combination of a young George Peppard and Truman Capote. He looks like a man who orders an Old Fashioned in a bar but has a flask in his Plymouth Fury. He's one UNC undergraduate generation away from farming. He knows how to ride a horse. He has a sister with two first names, and one of them is Mary. Most of his shoes can be worn without socks.

"No, it was that last one that rode the motorcycle. That's how he got killed, in the motorcycle accident. She cried and cried like—well, I hadn't never seen nothing like it. I never seen a woman act like that."

Granny didn't always act like a regular woman.

"It's like Alice said to me one time—you remember Alice from Archer Lodge who used to clean the house. 'You got that old graveyard love,' she said to me, talking about your father. 'You got that kinda love what you gone follow him till they put him in the ground. Then you gone go to the ground he in and keep on loving.'"

I remembered Alice, and I remembered my father, and I'm guessing Alice meant "you might put him in the graveyard yourself." I've seen love, but not between my parents. They were like two people who quit having fun playing Chinese checkers with each other hours ago but who had committed to a death match. So, that was fun to watch. Finally she gave up first. Turns out that was how you win at that particular Chinese checkers, but it had been a long time since anyone had checked the rulebook, evidently. Maybe Alice was talking about other people entirely. Mom gets the details mixed up sometimes. That sentence is really too pretty to be about my parents.

The story of Granny's last affair always came out of Mom in a great puff of offended wonder. "I thought we were gone have to put her in the state home. She didn't come out of her room. She wouldn't eat. His family wouldn't let her come to the funeral, of course."

On that sign outside Holy Family, where Granny's husband is buried:

Photography is not permitted in the cemetery. You must be a family member to visit. Please bring a birth certificate.

"You couldn't even talk to her. She was wild-like after that. I looked up one night and she was standing in the doorway to our bedroom, with that dog on a leash. That crazy one that bit you. Snarling and biting. Said she was gonna turn it loose on me. I still don't know what she was saying—she wasn't making no sense. Crying and moaning. We got ready to leave the house to go someplace on time around then, and there she sat. She'd taken all my wedding china out of the sideboard and laid it out on the dining room table. 'Y'all walk out that door,' she said, 'and I'll break every piece.' I swear I couldn't tell if she wanted to die or if she wanted to kill the rest of us for still being here."

That was not a bad way to put it. Except I never heard Granny say "y'all."

"He was so young—I didn't ever see what he saw in her. Young guy, not bad looking. Worked on cars. He probably wasn't too smart. Hilda reading all them books, I don't know what she saw in him, either. Just lonely, I guess."

I guess. A good-looking motorcycle-riding young man in 1962. And I've seen pictures of Granny back then. Also, she could flat tell a joke better than anybody I've ever met.

"With him, I guess it was a mother-figure thing." Mom squints and tilts her head at her own observation.

I can't wholly agree. Short of, say, the beasts of the wild who actually eat their young, Granny might have been the least maternal thing walking this world—men included.

"She never had another one after him, though. So either it was true love, or she was just worn out with them by then."

Mom doesn't believe in true love, it's worth noting.

I have a tiny copy of *Sonnets from the Portuguese* with an inscription to her from a man I never heard her mention. One of those vest-pocket editions, skinny so you could carry it with your pen. There have got to be people waiting for her. There has got to be a whole party on a big front porch, with hundreds of matchbooks waiting to light her cigarette. I just hope nothing I'm doing is holding her up. In this picture, the post holds her up, right at the edge of the frame, so her body almost leans out at you. Her head tilts to one side, the frames of her cat's eye glasses make it hard to see exactly where she's looking, but it looks like she's looking up. I let her go. I told her I would be all right. I hope that was enough.

I know what I did mattered, and not just for the effort, the attempt to bring my first son, into this world. I knew he was going to die in those two months, and so did he. Mother's Day happened to fall a few weeks before I went into labor. I spent most of the day alone with him, thinking very little. Driving around, I stopped and went into a bookstore, the kind of generic chain bookstore I usually avoided, with its sad piles of remainders and their black armbands. A store employee, an older woman, was walking around with a big basket of flowers, handing them out to the women with children. As usual, I forgot how obvious it was to everyone else that I was pregnant.

She startled me a little when I turned around, but she handed me a robust red carnation and smiled. "Happy Mother's Day!" she said.

I've never been good at the spontaneous polite lie. I'd buy extra to have them on hand, if you could pull off that kind of thing.

"I'm not a mother," I said back to her. I said it nicely. Well, as nicely as all the implied realities could have allowed such a statement to be.

This world's capacity for subtlety disappoints more often than not. But all of a sudden, I saw a hardiness in this little old woman that bolstered me on one of the worst days of my life. "You will be," she said, grabbing my arm. When I remember her, I don't remember her saying that part out loud. But it was clear as could be to me. She couldn't know the particulars, but she didn't need to. She saw us together, and in her I can remember how real he was. Mostly her, and Dr. McMahon. Nobody else knew us together. And nobody knew him but me. Not here, anyway.

Who were our friends? Who knew us together? What did they see, and did they know how I wronged him? Because he's here waiting to be brought over, one more time, and by me. He's here for me to finish this, what happened between us. And more and more, I have come to understand that he gave me this chance. He didn't do this—I did. It was me. I called him here. I'm that far, and even though there's more to understand, I hope he sees me and that he knows I haven't stopped thinking about him. That I didn't go merrily along with life after him without remembering. He wasn't just a moment of light, gone in the wash of the next bright day. I'm going to get to the bottom of it all. I hope it doesn't take too very long. And I hope it's beautiful where he is.

I still haven't gotten out all of George and Vivian. Thomas tells me that I should go ahead and explain these things to people, that if I give them the appropriate context, that they will hear these stories and understand. I'm trying to do that now.

I met George first. I still think I only know Vivian through George's memory of her. That would explain some of it, at least. He caught me by the arm that day in my friend's apartment. I was helping decorate for a Christmas party. Then, electricity from my elbow to my fingertips. And he started telling me about her first—

"The old lady next door, she's afraid of electricity. She covers up all the outlets in the apartment with heavy tape, and she calls me over to help her change the light bulbs. She holds a cup over the socket when she takes out the bulb, and I hand her the fresh one. She thinks while the socket's open that electricity is spilling out into the room and that somebody'll get shocked later when they run into it. I hold onto her kitchen chair so she doesn't fall. She's crazy. But I'd be sad if she got hurt. She reminds me of my mother. She doesn't have anybody else.

"I think she might have been a singer, one time. Like in nightclubs, or maybe even the movies. She has a gramo-phone, and a bunch of old records. I can hear her playing them at night when I come in sometimes, but she doesn't ever have them out when I come over. There are a bunch of old black-and-white pictures—I think one or two of them might be her, when she was really young, maybe. The dresses are fancy, spangled and feathered. Like pictures in old magazines.

"She had a cat one time. It used to come up to her window on the fire escape, because she'd feed it little pieces of fish. But she made me take it to my girlfriend. She said she couldn't have animals. That it hurt too much when they died, and that she just wanted it gone so it would stop looking at her. My girlfriend named the cat Demian because she reads a bunch of Hesse. Anyway, she's not my girlfriend anymore now, but I guess that cat is okay. The old lady loved the cat. She'd have probably taken care of it if I had just left it with her in the first place, but she cried and cried and begged me to take it, so I did because she was kind of killing me. She was breaking my heart.

"One day she knocked on my door and handed me this envelope. It was full of all those tags, you know, on pillows, the ones that say 'Do Not Remove Under Penalty of Law.' And there was a signed confession in there, too, that she was the one who had removed them because they cluttered up the place. I liked the letter. She was kind of unapologetic about the whole thing, and when you think about it, she's not wrong—those tags are kind of stupid."

"George!" said Vivian. "I swear, you'll talk to anybody."

Is she talking to me? Or is that still George, dazzled and electric, crackling through despite everything—

Chapter Eighteen

So of course after I met the first sister that day on Morrow Mountain, I went to Wilson Library at UNC, up to the Southern Historical Collection. I had spent a lot of time in that room reading letters when I was writing my dissertation. The ritual of locking up your bags, handing over your writing implements, verifying your identity—it gets you ready to travel backwards into the past. When you cross over, they give you a pencil and a magnifying glass. That's all you're going to need.

The two girls don't know anything about what's coming. A war and a new South. There's desire, though, and so there's movement. They've never been anyplace yet, and their books are the only way they'd know anything else exists. They're too young, yes. But old enough to stretch and fret between the town and the mountain, the only places they've ever seen...

I'm touching her notebooks, tracing the loops of her handwriting with my finger. I want it to tell me I'm right. But it's not likely to tell me anything I don't already know. This is fact-checking, that's all. These two sisters loved each other, and they twined themselves together like two trees in a myth...

The watercolor tins won't balance on the stump, and the cat keeps stepping in the can of water. She knows the red is not dark enough, not orange enough. The tomatoes go from golden yellow on the one side to a deep orange on the other. But Lizzie likes this shade, kind of puce. Which is a terrible sounding word, she thinks, but a nice shade. She'd like to have a dress this color. Or a dress with flowers this color—that would be better for a girl her age. She'd despise an orange dress. Or a dress with tomatoes on the trim! That's probably what she'd end up with.

"Addie, this cat."

"Lizzie, don't be a baby. Just nudge her. Make that sneezing noise—she hates that."

"She's up under me, and there she goes to the easel—now she's turned the whole thing over! It's ruined. Everything is ruined."

"It's not ruined, don't fuss so. See, you should have dug a hole for it to prop. If you're going to work out here in the garden, you've got to set up first."

Lizzie was almost done painting the infernal tomato plants. She left the book open for the page to dry in the sun. It was streaked of course, because of the stupid cat.

"You didn't put the blossoms on," Addie said.

"There aren't any blossoms right now."

"But you have to include them—it's not a portrait, you know. And that color is—"

"Addie, you're making me more tired."

Lizzie stretched her legs out, her back up against the tree stump, and closed her eyes.

"You're not tired. You're—"

"Bored. I wasn't going to say it because you asked me not to. But Addie, I've gone so long without thinking I don't think I can think anymore. I do have a new theory, though."

Lizzie leaned around the stump to look at Addie, who had come over from the arbor, but was distracted by a little bit of movement on the ground. She glanced up to study Lizzie instead, waiting for this old game of petulance or insult to continue. Lizzie hadn't been happy since they'd been back at home. Addie kept waiting for her to come around, but their time at school had shown Lizzie too many things for the mountain to be enough anymore. And for Addie, there was so much work to do—she wished Lizzie would get her focus back, because she felt like she was taking it all upon herself these days.

"Well, since you asked," Lizzie said, "here is my theory: I stand in one place all day. I drink a little water once in a while, and though I turn my face to the sun in hopes of growing strong, my feet stay rooted to the earth."

She'd spent the whole day on the tomato plant—they hadn't even finished the herb chart, but she didn't want to be in the greenhouse, no, she insisted on being in the garden, so she skipped all the way to the tomato—

"Too much shade has made me smaller than I should have been," Lizzie continued. "I'll never bear fruit at this rate."

And at this rate, she'll be in the garden all week. The immature stages of the tomato will have to be penciled in...

"Addie! I can't move!"

"Lizzie! What?"

"I'm a plant. I can't move."

"Lizzie, stop playing. And don't startle me that way, please. It's not funny."

"I'm a plant. Weren't you listening at all? That's my theory. I'm going to write it down in my notebook with my other theories."

"What other theories?"

"I could have other theories. You wouldn't know. You might not."

"I expect I'd know. Whether I felt like knowing or not."

"You love me. I rescued you."

Addie smiled, because it was true. Lizzie rescued her. She told Lizzie so when she was a baby, and it was still true. The mountain gave Addie nearly everything she could have ever imagined wanting, but Lizzie opened up her heart. In her sister, Addie saw a world in flashes, lit by lightning. Everything looked better after Lizzie found it.

"I'm still the good sister," Addie warned.

Lizzie picked up her notebook and flapped the pages to dry them. She walked toward Addie, who had picked up a little brown beetle and was inserting it into one of the glass bottles she kept in her vest pocket. Lizzie reached out for the tiny, slender magnifying glass Addie wore on a silver chain and held it up so they could both look at the creature.

"You be the good sister, sweet one," she whispered. "I count on you for that, you know. And so does Daddy."

"Hm. What would you do if something happened to me?"

"Addie!" Lizzie's laughter stayed with Addie long after Lizzie had gone to the house.

"Don't you know? Nothing ever happens to us. Daddy's the doctor, after all. And we're the doctor's helpers."

I'm never leaving this mountain, Addie thought. But she shrugged it off, that feeling. She picked up Lizzie's paintbrushes and started to clean each one slowly, wiping it in the grass and drying it with the cloth. Then she carefully replaced each tin's cap before restoring it to its labeled spot in the box. She checked the notebook, finally, and pressed the dried pages flat before closing the binding. On the page before the tomato plant painting, she saw that Lizzie had painted a beautiful white horse. A young man was riding it, right out of the woods on the south end of the clearing. Oh, Lizzie, Addie thought, even father won't be able to stop you from leaving us.

I spend that whole afternoon with the girls, reading their lists, magnifying the curls of their script. When I collect my bags, my coat, and my computer from the reference librarian, I check my email. I've received a reply from Emiliano, my ancestral bridge. He seems like a nice man.

"Please if you could send the date for the emigration of your great-grandfather. If you have the date, it would be a big help."

In my files from the ancestry websites, I find the passenger list from the S.S. Cincinnatti, crossing from Naples in 1910. Nicola Fiore, thirty years old. No mention of his wife, and it says he was a farm worker, but he was a butcher. But it's him. It matches everything else. Scanning down the page lengthwise, I see the last column is a next-of-kin listing with his father's name: Gaetano. That's as far back as I've ever seen on that side of my family. Granny talked about her husband's parents a lot, but never their parents—just that they left their families in Italy. I could never even figure out whether my grandfather was born here. I still don't really know. Maybe Emiliano will locate some answers for me. It's a much more distant past I'm really hoping to connect with in Italy. I want to plant my feet on the land that nursed the brutal Samnites. I want some of that steely Irpinian fierceness. I'm looking for my tribe.

Nora's got some Irpinian fierceness. She's full of purpose, unstoppable. I bet if I were a box of pencils, she'd draw

a mural the size of a football field, if necessary, to use them
up. She'd draw all the things we love: llamas, tapirs, octopi
with intricate tentacles. She'd draw all of Seattle, especially
the Smith Tower and the corner of First and Seneca. She'd
draw teacups and coffee cups, every kind of noodle, piles of
fountain pens and typewriters, dismantled typewriters, letters
of the alphabet in every font and chopped up into piles of
serifs and swoops. She'd draw the Eiffel Tower and Il Duomo.
She'd draw John Singer Sargeant's *Madame X* and Edward Gorey's *Doubtful Guest*, and a host of Gorey Fantods. Sloths, hydrangeas, and Bells of Ireland, piles of leaves, a Shelby Cobra
like Steve McQueen had, multiple spacecraft, and pairs and
pairs of black boots. She'd draw me, and she'd draw Granny,
and she'd draw her brothers. She'd draw Thomas. She already
drew me this great picture of Edgar. Anyway, she wouldn't
be freaked out. She'd just get to work. That's the wolf-girl in
her. The tribe who sacrificed its firstborn males in the rough
years.

I'll ask her about the pencils sometime. I'm not worried
about it. Right now she's painting me a fox reading a book.
He's wearing a beautiful kimono. The sky is the color of hydrangeas. We understand each other perfectly.

$\frac{1}{7}$

*I think it's snowing. Something is wet on my face. I don't think I'm breathing
at all anymore. But I can still hear my heart beating, and I can still hear the
tinkling of their little bells, the beasts. Or their chains. The stars are closer, too,
now. Maybe the beasts are looking up at them with me.*

Chapter Nineteen

HOW DO YOU KNOW who is important in your life? Besides your parents and your children, the line of humans to which you belong—but there are other kinds of love that pull all of us together. Sometimes at great speed and against sense. We could be romantic about it and believe it's left over from another time, some kind of eternal love that is stronger than the separation of death. We could be superstitious about it and cross ourselves, perform the rituals that will protect us from the clinging needs of the dead. Or we can listen to the stories that persist. We can note the signal fires. We can tell each other stories against the darkness.

In 1988, a young man met an old woman. He drew close to her. He thought it might have something to do with his past. All stories—and it's important to know this—all stories are love stories.

"Vivian? Are you home? I got your note about the light..."

George knocked again. He always wondered if she'd gone completely deaf. She always said she couldn't hear out of her left ear, but to him it seemed like she might not hear at all lately. She knew what you were saying if she could see your face when you were talking. He figured she'd just gradually learned to read lips. Maybe she didn't even realize how deaf she was. But lately, every time she left a message for him to come by, she'd leave her door a little bit open so she'd know when he got there. It worried him. The building was pretty safe, but you never knew who might be around. If he didn't make it home one night, and she fell asleep...

"Georgie boy."

He heard her, somewhere in there, so he walked on into the foyer, out into the middle of the oriental rug. Staring straight up, he could see all three bulbs were out in her hall fixture.

The first time he met her, she asked him to help her hold the ladder. He wondered how long those things must have been out before she found somebody to stand there while she fixed it. Good thing she didn't break her leg in the dark hallway. At least she didn't try to do it herself; even she wasn't that stubborn. The hall ceiling was a good two feet higher than the living room, one of the quirks of the old building that he liked, along with the twisting halls and the oddly shaped rooms. The whole building was somebody's house once, some old robber baron, probably. Back when this part of New York was the suburbs.

George liked to visit Vivian for a lot of reasons. She had a great collection of old records. Seemed like she had been friends with a bunch of old musicians, some that he knew and some he'd never even heard of. Old pictures showed her on the bandstand in velvet and satin, making that same face of mock surprise, like she was about to whistle low. She'd do that when he told her about his day, things that happened at work, and the occasional gigs he had, though he hadn't been playing much lately. She especially made that face when he talked about a girl, even if it was just a friend of his.

"Don't you want to get married?" she'd ask him. "You're gonna get old, you know. You'll look up one day and it'll happen. Then you're gonna want somebody so you don't have to drink all by yourself. You're not supposed to do that."

And then the face, both sour and puss, but a joke all the same.

"I do it anyway," she'd whisper. He liked her carelessness. She knew it was okay for her not to care, and she reveled in it.

But he was glad when she'd ask him to help her with the light. Every time he saw it, it bothered him. He tried to talk her into replacing it with one easier to deal with—he even offered to put it in, one that would hang lower.

"That lamp is the real thing," she'd say. "It's been in this house longer than we have. It belongs to this house, not to me or to you. It stays right where it is."

"Well, at least get a floor lamp and let it go out. You won't need it if you just put a couple over here..."

"No, Georgie—look at it. It's like a face if you stand up underneath. It's got two eyes and a little round mouth. And when you light it up, it's as pink as a peach!"

George was pretty sure he'd read someplace that mentally ill people often saw faces in unexpected places, inanimate objects with patterns, like wallpaper. Or oriental rugs like the one he was standing on. Or lamps, he guessed.

"Don't give it a face, Vivian. I don't want to have to feel sorry for it. I don't like it. If it's some kinda thing with a face, I don't want to have to worry about what it's up to."

"You worry too much. Most things won't take much care, you know. Most people won't either. You've got to love them just enough without breaking them."

She'd say the same thing each time, extracting each flame-shaped bulb one at a time, placing them in the bowl George held in one hand while he held the ladder with the other. They had the system down. She had the bowl and the bulbs on the hall table waiting for him.

He was staring up at the dark face in the ceiling when she came out of the kitchen. "I made us a snack," she said.

"Olives?"

"Olives for you. And I had some Huntsman cheese. And some pound cake. First let's get out of the dark."

"Where's the ladder?"

"Let me get it—I had to take it over to the bathroom, because the shower curtain was coming down in the back—"

"I didn't know about that—did you come by? Why didn't you let me help—"

"You don't need to help with everything, Georgie boy, and anyway you were out with ah, your new little friend, miss—"

"Oh, last Friday. Sharon."

"Sharon. Miss Sharon," she glanced over her shoulder and made the lemon face, raising her eyebrows high. She still kept them in a wide arch, like a film star.

"You like this one," she said. "Don't look so stricken. It's no shame in loving somebody. Is she gonna fall like a peach?"

"Give me the ladder, hey."

"All right, take it, Mr. Bones. You can have it." She heaved out a big sigh and straightened her back. George set the feet of the ladder on the big hibiscus flowers on the rug. That was the middle, straight under the lamp. He looked up to check. Perfect.

"Ready, Mr. Bones? I'm going up. Don't let me fall and die, why don't you. Because I'm gonna die alone. I got it all planned."

No one with a name dies alone.

Chapter Twenty

"Just don't stage an intervention or anything. Give me a warning or something. I'm working on it, you know."

Thomas thinks it's getting to me, the weight of the ashes.

"That's what I'm saying—I'll go with you to look at a mausoleum if you want. There're other places besides that one where your mom has—what—how many plots does she have? Seriously, does she just buy one next to everybody she likes a lot to cover her bases? How many people think they're spending eternity with her?"

"After what I've been trying to figure out, I'm not giving anybody a hard time about their plans. Perhaps she has intentions to be divided—"

Thomas held up both hands like a mime. "That," he said, "I will not get behind."

"Well, I doubt that's the instruction. But nothing surprises me anymore."

"We both agree she probably needs to... go."

"Yes. We agree."

"And I'm asking here, because when we got married, I knew she was gonna be in the house, and I was good with that."

"Well, I did warn you. I appreciate that everybody has indulged my intention to keep her. My previous intention—I don't think I thought it through. People are not décor."

I got distracted, because I'm pretty sure Granny convinced me at one point that after Roy Rogers had Trigger stuffed and displayed in his house that he expressed an intention to do the same thing with sweet blonde Dale, should she be the first to pass over.

"She just, she just said she wanted to be cremated. I never asked 'WHAT THEN?'"

"Before the last few weeks, I would've said, 'Why the hell would she?' She's dead, she doesn't care. But I operate on evidence, and the evidence says she needs to be someplace else."

We sat there, the wretched urn perched on the sideboard like a pound cake waiting for dinner to be over.

"Don't get me wrong. Shit does not scare me. But your car ignition—I changed that battery myself. The closet door—I can't shut it enough times. And I've had it with the light bulbs. That may just be you. Either way, your stress gets high, I'm buying bulbs once a week and I never get off the fucking ladder."

"I know."

"She's not hurting anything. But she's got someplace else to be. Isn't that what she used to say to you?"

Granny could smell a pity visit. So she thought—they weren't pity visits, strictly speaking. I've been afraid all my life of the day she'd die and leave me. Every time I saw her in those last few years, I'd watch her standing on the sidewalk as I drove away, thinking the next time I saw her she might be in a hospital or dead already.

And who the fuck OD's on Tylenol PM?

"I was bored," she told me, in the hospital. "I can't read anymore, and TV makes no sense to me now."

In the facility, she was the biggest pain in the ass. Physically crippled but verbally sharp and fierce, she unleashed on anything that came close enough to hear.

"ARE YOU SLEEPING WITH HIM?" she shrieked at my mother and her attorney when they came to have her sign some papers regarding her will. She still believed she owned the house my father had stolen from her years before, and she wanted me to have it. The papers didn't mean anything, really, but they soothed her. Until something about poor James, the attorney, struck her. She was a sucker for a smart-looking man with nice eyewear.

"DIANE, YOU CAN TELL ME IF YOU'RE SLEEPING WITH HIM. I DON'T MIND." She leered at James. "MY SON IS A JACKASS!" she screamed at him. "SHE SHOULD FUCK SOMEONE NICE. YOU LOOK NICE." She gave him her Clara Bow innocent look, but since the fall, her muscle control was a little suspect so the effect was, well, kind of chilling.

"DIANE, HE'S SHORT, BUT HE'S GOOD LOOKING. COME OVER HERE CLOSER, MISTER! I like your LIPS."

"Should I go?" James offered.

"I think that might be for the best," I said, because James was about to hear more from a little old lady than he was used to, and it was time to wrap things up before they came in and shot her up with sedatives. She was getting excited, writhing around.

A few weeks later, I was trying to trim her fingernails in the sun room. The nurses had stopped doing it—I don't know if it was medication or what, but the old broad had started growing these impressive yellow pterodactyl talons that were an absolute panic to remove. Two old men were moving checkers pieces around. Another old woman was talking to herself. Well, she was talking to her daughter, who sounded like a raging bitch even though she wasn't there in the room to prove it.

"Helen, I understand if you don't want to talk to me. I think I was a disappointment to you. But why can't I see the children? You used to let me see the children sometimes, Helen. Helen, they said I can't have the cupcakes anymore, in the cafeteria they have cupcakes but they won't bring me one, Helen. I tried to call you, Helen, I haven't been able to talk to you in weeks and weeks, Helen. Helen? The children, Helen. Why can't I see them? Betty came last week, Helen, and she said she saw you in church. I'm praying for you, Helen."

I finally started offering an answer every once in a while.

"Thank you. Thank you for praying for me, Mother."

She stopped talking and looked around for a minute, but I don't think she saw me. I don't even know if the poor woman knew where she was. Honestly, I don't know who Helen is, whether she's her daughter or not, whether she's dead or alive.

"He-len?"

"Yes."

"Is that you?"

There was really nothing left to decide at that point.

"It's me."

"Helen. I always loved you, you know that."

"I know it. I love you, too."

She bent her head to the side, leaning over the arm of the wheelchair. Then she started to sob, little soft sobs. Granny was sobbing, too.

"You're hurting me, Ruth. Why are you hurting me? What did I ever do to you?"

She'd been calling me Ruth—her dead sister's name—for weeks, but that part was fine. She announced it. She said, I'm going to call you Ruth once in a while; I know you're not Ruth. Then she giggled that dirty-joke laugh. It just leveled her when Ruth died first—she kept going on about how Ruth was the baby. It was like the whole fucking world turned up-side down for her. Like she had a deal made, and somebody screwed it up. It was hard to be sympathetic, too, because I'd only met Ruth a few times—she moved north when she was in her early twenties and stayed—but every time I saw her, she was hard and bossy, like a human grudge.

And because Ruth had lived so far away for most of their adult lives, she'd forget every day that Ruth was already dead, and then she'd remember suddenly, and the whole thing would start up again. Every day she lived after Ruth, it was like she thought she was going to be charged extra on some kind of bill. I could never really understand that part, except that Granny was the oldest and Ruth was the youngest.

"Hilda, we've got to get these fingernails off of you," I pleaded on one especially bleak Sunday afternoon. "You're going to hurt yourself—look, now, if you jerk your hand like that I AM going to hurt you! Now you're bleeding! Look what you did!"

And then I started to sob. That was the worst. I think right then was worse than when she died, because I couldn't find her in all of that sadness and guilt.

I was still holding her hands when we both got too tired to cry anymore.

"You didn't have to sleep with him, Ruth. Why'd you sleep with him? I never had anything that was mine, you knew that."

Shit. Really? Fuck. My aunt was a crazy bitch for sure, but this part was news. She used to call up my dad in the middle of the night and yell at him. For crazy stuff, like cutting down trees or moving around boulders on the family farm. None of which had ever actually happened. Of all the things, all the messed-up stuff she could have been angry about, somehow it was always related to landscaping.

"Ruth!" I'd hear him shout while lying in my bed in the next room, usually around 3 a.m. "Ruth! Shut the fuck up, Ruth! You're a crazy bitch. I'm going back to sleep now. Don't fucking call me again."

Granny was still staring up at me in shock, waiting for an answer.

"Hilda, I am so sorry. If I were you, I would not forgive me."

I figured I'd better think this next part through a little bit, because while it might be entertaining to me to right a whole series of perceived wrongs, when you get those lightning intervals, those interstices where new realities and futures open up to you, you can't force too much into that space.

"But you were always so much more responsible and fair. I'm sorry. I am a careless person. You're worth ten of the rest of us."

I can't be sure she heard me. I can't be sure. But she leaned back, and she let me finish her nails. By the end, you couldn't cut them at all. You had to file them, and it took an awfully long time to do each little one. An awfully long time.

Thomas waits for an answer of some kind. He's been waiting a while. He doesn't need to know all these stories, but still he's been listening, cigarette by cigarette. I think he knows that I need to tell them. How long ago did he even ask me this question? It's a lot to ask of somebody, helping you dispose of a body.

Yeah, it's not exactly that, I know. But still.

"I think I have an idea, about the ashes. Just give me a few days."

"Baby, you can have all the time you need. Whatever it is you're planning, just let me know how to help. I will make some shit happen, you just tell me."

"Oh, I'm going to need your help. But I need to check out a few things first."

CHAPTER TWENTY-ONE

WILLIAM ACKLAND, SON OF TENNESSEE, buried in North
Carolina in the museum that bears his name on the campus
of the University of North Carolina's flagship campus in
Chapel Hill. He's really in there. Most people don't know
that. To be accurate: most people don't think about it.

I've only had Granny's ashes twelve years. I wonder where
they kept Ackland in the eighteen years between his death and
that day that John Larson arrived in Chapel Hill to explain
how he'd performed the legal magic to plant an art museum
and a good-hearted—if slightly mysterious—benefactor just
around the corner from the bars and restaurants and student
shenanigans on Franklin Street.

I go over to the Ackland every chance I get. There's an il-
luminated page from a Medieval Book of Hours I like to visit.
A Corot I wrote a paper about when I was an undergrad in a
big Art History survey course. Sometimes there's a concert
or a particular exhibit—there's lot of good museums around
these days, but the special appeal of the tiny Ackland is its
quirky sensibility. And its permanent resident. I always end
up going to see him.

I was standing next to the tomb, by the effigy's feet, tucked
into the alcove where he's set around the corner from the
entrance. I flatten myself tight to the wall when the school
groups come by.

And here we have a loving tribute to our founder, William
Ackland. On September 20, 1958, this museum was dedi-
cated to the betterment of future generations of the students
of this University and inhabitants of the town." The docent

points out a couple of photos helpfully placed alongside the crypt, one of the crowded dais on dedication day, one a portrait of Ackland in his youth.

"Is he really in there?" There's always that one kid. Always. I try to keep out of it, but when the docents don't want to talk about it...

"I don't think so, dear. It's just a tribute..."

"Oh, he's in there. That was part of the deal." There's no point really in shielding them from the realities of life and death. They're in an art museum.

"Really? Well, how come it says he died in 1940, but they didn't build this place until..." Oh good; this kid can count.

"As with most estates of the wealthy and unmarried, disputes had arisen. The path to the resolution of Ackland's will and the final location of his remains had been winding its way to Chapel Hill since his sudden death in 1940. Mr. Ackland's wishes had been ultimately defended by the shrewd legal mind of John E. Larson, who found in the Ackland case what would be the distinguishing moment of his career. "

If you go to Chapel Hill in the full beauty of its October, you'll return again. That's what they say, anyway. Late September can still be hot and humid. It all depends. Twilight mosquitoes. Frogs still croaking in the arboretum. I don't know what the weather was like in 1958, but it was probably something like that.

"Cool, there's a dead guy in there."

Kid, you're right. It's very cool that a dead guy is in there. It's a good story.

But it's not a ghost story. I had been reading about Ackland, whatever little I could find, since I found the museum when I was about sixteen or so. I figured it was about the best case of estate planning ever. Now all I could think was, how can I do this? Can I build a palace of Victorian novels and dirty jokes to house Hilda's ashes?

And what was the afterlife like for Ackland? I don't think Larson spent a lot of time thinking about that part. Maybe Ackland listens with the matrons who attend the Sunday afternoon lectures. Maybe he floats among the donors at the exhibit openings, sipping their cocktails while they are distracted. Or maybe on Thursday nights, he sneaks out of his tomb, sweeping his cloak around himself, slipping past the guard and heading down to Frankin Street to He's Not Here. Maybe he sniffs the necks of curly-headed boys swatting away mosquitoes, drinking Rolling Rock, feeling a static in the air and seeing the late-summer haze halo the sputtering streetlamps that light up their young skins with the glow of a very old kind of love.

That's one afterlife I can imagine.

So I've explained my idea to Thomas. He's a better strategist. He also thinks that with enough time, space and money, you can build a rocket to Mars. I think that's reaching. Sometimes it's okay to reach, and I don't actually need to go to Mars this time.

"No, I think it's a great idea. Let me think. I hear you, yeah, it's... it's good. I like it. I can see why you would, and I can see how she would—how you could let this be the thing, you know, that feels like doing right by her."

I like my idea, but I'm still not sure it can be fully implemented. But Thomas's enthusiasm has me excited. "You see what I mean. You can't just ask for something like this."

"Oh, you could ask. But you might have trouble getting a 'yes' out of somebody. I mean, to me and you, it's not a big thing. But some people might find it..."

"Ghoulish."

"Maybe. Or just, not an idea to which they are easily accustomed. Most people do just get buried in the ground, the regular way. That's pretty much our cultural procedure. That's the deal most people feel like they've got. But don't think for a moment I'm saying you've got to settle for that. I didn't know her, but after your stories and, well, living with her for these few years, I'm feeling oddly invested in her eternal happiness as well. And I think this sounds pretty good. We might have to get a little creative with the execution."

"I don't really have a problem with that."

"No. I didn't expect you would."

There are all kinds of places—and not just crypts or mausoleums—where human remains have been interred. And certainly there have been people who have gone to their final resting place surrounded by things they love—and not just pharaohs.

"There was a guy who got buried in his vintage car. And another one in his favorite recliner... And the Ackland dude—the one Duke wouldn't bury in the museum so they turned down his endowment, so UNC popped up and said, 'Hey y'all, we're a state school, and we're not squeamish. Haul him on up in here.'" I've been doing a lot of research about this kind of thing.

"Oh yeah—that really is him in there, isn't it? You told me that, I remember. That's one hell of a headstone."

"See, I bet you there is a library someplace with somebody in it. It seems completely natural to me. If I won the lottery, I'd just build one myself."

"Yeah, well. We might not need the lottery to make this work. I think we just need to do a little research. Are you going to be okay if this isn't, let's say, the most delicate operation?"

"One can find dignity in many ways." I believe that's true, yes.

"All right then. Operation Relocation begins. Unless you tell me different."

My one condition was that I really preferred that it be within a day's drive. I wanted to be able to visit once in a while still.

Granny worked in a library when she was a young woman. The Olivia Raney Library in old downtown Raleigh, with Mrs. Atkinson, who was only the second librarian ever to be there. It was a serious place, the beginning of the Wake County library system, the first place to have a children's section or to be open on Sundays. That had been a big discussion, opening on Sundays. For Granny, there was no more sacred space than a library. If she were being honest about her chosen place of worship, the library would have been it.

She met "the Grand Old Man" there, one of her admirers. She never said his name, just called him "the Grand Old Man," or "the Governor." I don't think he was ever really the governor. Maybe a politician. But I sure have entertained myself pondering which one he might have been.

Between checking out books in the library and cashiering at the diner across from the college, Granny must have met nearly everyone in Raleigh. But she wasn't at the library to meet the people. Not the living ones, anyway.

I gave her a whole set of Brontë books one Christmas, then a set of Trollope for her birthday, which was twelve days later on old Christmas. She called me up a few days later.

"I feel like I've been on a trip with a bunch of old friends that I hadn't seen in a long time."

"You read those before?"

"I read everything in the Olivia Raney library."

That was always the answer in every book discussion. If I had a list of the books in the Olivia Raney library, I could pretty much tell you everything she ever read.

"Even the bad ones. They're not all good, you know. But I never met one I didn't like, at least a little bit."

Granny would have liked people better if they had all just told better stories.

But anyway it hit me that day, driving past the Olivia Raney library (which is still there, miraculously existing as a genealogical research library)—that's the happiest she ever was. Young, unattached, spending her days in a sea of books, with a woman whose mission it was to improve the lot of her Southern cohorts by bringing them the Word, or the words—the other ones.

"Okay," I said to Thomas, back at the computer, "so I googled North Carolina new library construction. There's a swamp of information about the new James B. Hunt library over at State. That thing must be something. There's like a gazillion articles…"

"Well, that ship has sailed. Unless we drop her down a ventilation shaft or something."

"That'll never do. What if somebody found it and removed it? No telling where she'd end up. I can just see her sitting there, with that big old purse in her lap. Waiting for somebody to drive her home."

"You do remember she's in that box over there. No sitting. No purse."

"I'm just saying. She still has her same manner of being. Coffee cup and a cigarette in one hand, tin pan of cat food in the other. Sneaking around in her foam slippers. Or a beer can and a cigarette in one hand and a book in the other."

"So did you find anything?"

"Oh. Yeah, actually—there was a bond referendum in Forsythe County, and evidently they are building three new libraries within the year. I'm having trouble finding the exact locations."

"That sounds promising."

"Might take a while. There is one that's adding a North Carolina collection to its existing library. But it sounds like it's a little more geared toward historical documents and whatnot. I'd like to get her close to some books."

"What about this? Click on that one."

"Oh, yeah. That's not bad. That could work."

"If we time it right..."

"Looks like we could maybe... put her in the foundation. Is that bad? It sounded bad out loud. I mean, would a wall be better? Like the House of Usher. She loved that story."

"I don't see anything particularly wrong with putting her in the foundation. What's the difference with a wall or the foundation? It's not like—I mean, she's ashes, Nicole. It's less weird than catacombs."

"We'd have to get some plans. I don't want her ending up under the second stall in the men's room."

"Are you kidding? From your descriptions..."

"Okay, yeah, that might not be so bad. Let's make sure she's not in the parking garage at least."

I want to bury my face in their furry necks and feel their sharp teeth sink into me. I hear their paws breaking the surface of the snow, each little crunch. We'll be one beast then, and we'll be able to fly out of here, off this glacier and up into the stars. A brother to Ptolemy's Lupus. Another sacrifice. I try to howl, but nothing. Just the ice in my throat.

CHAPTER TWENTY-TWO

"VIVIAN, YOU DON'T HAVE ANY COFFEE—but you've got about forty dollars in quarters in the coffee pot-shaped jar that says 'Coffee' on it."

"Look in the flowerpot."

"The flowerpot? The flowerpot is full of flowers. And dirt. Vivian, I had no idea this was how you made coffee. This changes everything, you know."

Vivian came into the kitchen holding an ancient Bergdorf's bag by the handles with both hands.

"Not the flowerpot. The flour pot—right next to the one that says 'Coffee'—"

George lifted the latch on the canister and began spooning coffee into the percolator.

"What do I need flour for? What am I gonna bake? I put the coffee in the biggest one. I don't want to run out. And I got the quarters in case I need to make a phone call."

"That's a lot of phone calls."

"I know a lotta people. When I die, I'm gonna have to let a lotta people know."

"Life's one big challenge to logic for you, isn't it, Vivian?"

"I yam what I yam. That's what the sweet potato said to Popeye."

George had gotten used to spending Sunday mornings with Vivian. It was a hard thing to explain sometimes, especially on Saturday night.

"No, I really need to go home. I'll call you Tuesday before I come to pick you up."

"You know, it stinks that you won't stay the night. It's selfish. You know it makes me feel cheap, and you do it anyway. I don't even think this old broad is real. You said your mother was dead!"

They never understood, the girls, that it was a bad gambit to talk about George's mother. His mother was dead, and that's all he felt like saying. He didn't feel like explaining how all of his memories of her were chunks of time chopped with his father's stopwatch. The doctor supervising his wife's care. And it was always time to go; you could beg for maybe ten more minutes. Okay, two more minutes. He remembered picking up her hand and the shock of static, probably from the soft slippers she wore, crossing the big oriental rugs in the visiting room. She usually didn't notice, the sedation was so heavy. It was the only way he could visit. As plaintive as he was in his requests to stay, her abject sorrow at his every departure threatened the continuation of any visits at all. So she agreed to heavy sedation. He held her hands and stared at her sleepy smile. Sometimes he'd crawl into her lap. A few weeks before he turned ten, his father came into his room one morning before church.

"Your mother has died. You should wear your black suit to church today."

And he didn't see her again. No funeral, as far as he knew. He wasn't even sure where she was buried.

CHAPTER TWENTY-THREE

MY DAD HAD A FAVORITE TRICK. In retrospect, I find it hard
to believe this is one of Vaughn's. But everybody has their
flaws, their moments of contemptible weakness. This trick
depended entirely on me, and I hated it. From age eight or
nine on. I think he tried to pull this crap as late as 1984, but
I'm pretty sure I had started just hanging up on him by then.

That day the Mike Douglas show was on, and I'd curled up
in the ugly green recliner with a bowl of Cheetos, the puffed
ones. When the phone started ringing in the kitchen, I re-
luctantly crawled out, put my bowl carefully in the seat, and
trotted over while licking the orange cheesy powder off my
right hand. I jumped up on the barstool to reach it, probably
between the seventh and eighth ring.

"Hello?"

"Yes! Good afternoon. With whom am I speaking? I am
with, ah, Jack Spencer, and I would like to speak to Mr. Wizard."

"Aw, Dad, come on..."

"It's me, yes. I would LIKE to SPEAK to Mr. Wizard. If
it's a convenient time."

"Please don't make me do this again, Dad. I hate this. I
feel stupid, and I don't—"

"Just ask Mr. Wizard. I am CERTAIN he is WELL AC-
QUAINTED with me. WELL. ACQUAINTED."

"Arright, arright."

I mumbled, sighed, and started licking the rest of the orange cheesy powder still left on my hands.

Smacking, I started. "Two, three, four, five, six, seven, eight, nine—"

"Very well! Yes! Thank you so much for your help!"

"Nine?"

"Ahem."

"Is that a yes?"

"Yes—They're putting me on hold for him—it'll be just a moment—"

"Hearts. Spades. Diamonds. Clubs."

"Mr. Wizard!"

"Clubs?"

"Yes, Mr. Wizard, to you as well! Mr. Wizard, I have someone I'd like to introduce to you, if I might—let me put him on the line..."

There was some crackling and breathy shuffling, then a new voice.

"Um, hello? This is Jack Spencer. Nice to meet—"

"YOUR CARD IS THE NINE OF CLUBS. WALK WITH THE LIGHT."

If I had to do this stupid trick, I wanted my own tagline or catchphrase. Dad would never hear it, anyway. Heck, after hearing their card, the guys were usually whooping and swearing, so I'm not sure they heard it, either. I tried "Peace Be With You" at first, because that's my favorite part of mass. But it seemed a little benign as a request from an omniscient wizard with a secretary. Well, maybe not omniscient. All he ever did was tell people what card they'd pulled out of a fresh Bi-

cycle pack. Now if Mr. Wizard had been a benevolent, omniscient wizard, his tagline would have been "I See Loss Coming
For You," or "Don't Bet it All, Pilgrim." Last time we were
going to Hudson Belk's downtown for shoes, I saw a sign at
the street corner. It said "Walk With the Light," and I thought
Hey, if the guy on the other end had any brains at all, those
words ought to have had the same benevolent effect. But by
the time a guy in a back room of a steakhouse in Goldsboro is
on the phone with Mr. Wizard, his goose is pressure-cooked.

"Still there, Mr. Wizard? We'll talk when I get home."

"He seems nice. Leave him enough to get home, why don't
you."

I didn't say the last part out loud. Neither did Mr. Wizard.
Mr. Wizard's got a bowl of Cheetos, and Henry Kissinger's
on Mike Douglas.

CHAPTER TWENTY-FOUR

"HOW'S MISS BEVERLY this morning?"

"She's not here."

"She's gone? Where'd she go?"

"Yes. She's not here."

"Did she travel in her Estate Wagon?"

Miss Beverly drives a Buick Roadmaster Estate Wagon. Edgar has been clear and consistent on this point.

"Yes, she did. She did. "

I have no fucking clue what a Buick Roadmaster Estate Wagon looks like. Nor do I know how or why or how my three-year-old got to be an expert on them.

Edgar still had on his pajama shirt, and I had stopped chasing him, waiting instead on the monkey chair for him to wander within arm's length so I could stick him in a sweater.

"Is Miss Beverly okay? How's she doing? She's not... un-happy?"

"She'll be back."

"Oh, okay. So she still likes us. She's not mad."

"Yes, yes. She's not mad. She had to go on a trip. For a little while."

"Well that's certainly interesting."

"Hm. I'm fixing. I got to fix."

Edgar looked at me like I must be easily amused or some-thing. He was wrestling with a toy set of channel locks, a stuffed giraffe and the Blue Chair's leg. That's evidently what the "fixing" involved. The Blue Chair was Thomas's grandmother's. We'd put it in Edgar's room when he was an infant because it was comfortable, wide and armless—I liked it for nursing. Then it became, like most bedroom chairs, a stuffholder rather than a seat. I was getting ready to move it back downstairs about the time he started talking. And then one day, he told us about the lady who sat in it.

"She's old. She's... she's... a lady in the chair. She sit in it. While I'm sleeping."

So I don't mess with the chair. As long as he's in good stead with the lady who protects him while he sleeps, it stays. Edgar's fixing it. He's got it under control.

"WHAT'S THAT?" Edgar has dropped the channel locks but still has a strong hold on the giraffe by its throat. Every time he swings to the right to face the bedroom door, the giraffe makes its internal magic wand-swoosh noise.

"What's what? That noise? It's maagiiic..."

"No no no. Not the giraffe sound. What's that."

He's really not asking me. The first time I saw him dart out like that into the hallway on high alert, he stared down to the end of the tile path at the far bedroom door and shouted "Jesus! Jesus!" When I told him not to say that word that way, he clarified: "No, there's Jesus. Hi. Hi, Jesus. It's Jesus and the Cubble."

Jesus and the Cubble appeared regularly, if not frequently, at the end of the of the hallway, between the thresholds of the two rooms on the end of the house. I was still at loose ends as to what the Cubble was. It was a slightly more mysterious figure than Jesus, who seemed entirely benevolent, just checking in on us, maybe gathering some intel or something. He often exited through the shower in our bedroom. The Cubble, according to Edgar, both was and was not human in form, and both was and was not the same thing as Jesus. Got that? Yeah. We're not religious people. Not yet anyway. A few more episodes like these, and I'm not making promises.

This time though he was more agitated. And so was I, after realizing that I had also darted out into our hallway and asked my three-year-old, with great excitement, whether Jesus had come back.

"No. No. It's not Jesus. Don't you see them? They are RIGHT THERE."

Whoever it was, they were at our end of the hallway. Right at the bottom of the stairs. Edgar crouched at the top of the stairs and pointed to the bottom step, thrusting his index finger for emphasis.

"DON'T YOU SEE THEM!"

"Sweetie, I don't! I can't see them—can you tell me what they look like?"

"The people! It's the people, and they, they are jumping up and down. They JUMP. JUMP!" Edgar hopped a couple of times, his elbows bent, hands balled up in fists at his waist. He looked over at me. I wasn't sure if I should jump or tell a lie.

"Tell me more, because I don't see them. YOU see them, but I can't. Are they okay?"

"I don't know. They are all jumping on one foot, all the people. They have to jump on one foot. They have to."

Then he looked up really sadly at me, like he wanted me to help them out with this one-foot thing.

"I don't know, baby. Why do they have to jump on one foot?"

He sighed. "I... do... not... know." Still staring at the bottom step, he reached over for my hand. "You come. Come with me."

We walked over and started down the steps. Edgar stopped at each one and leaned over like he was listening.

One morning, when I was a kid and only a year or two older than Edgar is now, I jumped out of bed excited because I heard my cousin Dusty's voice in the house. I ran all around, but I found that not only was there no Dusty, but there was nobody. I was completely alone. I didn't know where anyone was. I started to cry. It was early, still misty outside when I ran out in bare feet and my white nightgown. I ran around in the wet grass. My parents' cars were both gone. I ran back into the house, through it, through the voice I was still hearing but I knew wasn't Dusty at all. "DON'T LOOK AT ME!" I yelled at it. "DON'T MAKE ME SEE YOU!"

I ran out the back door to my grandmother's apartment, which extended in an L off the end of our house. I flung open her screen door. It was dark inside, and the wooden door was locked. She was gone, too. I banged and banged on the door until it flew open. There she was, head full of pink curlers, still half asleep.

"Jesus, Mary and Joseph," she said, taking the toothpick out of her mouth. "You're going to catch something and die."

"I heard Dusty. Where's Dusty?"

"You were dreaming, that's all. You dreamed it."

"No! I heard Dusty. Didn't you hear them?"

"Who else is here?"

"Nobody. I can't find them."

"You're all wet. Nicky, shit. Sit down. Put this on. My Jesus. You're gonna be sick."

"I'm sorry I woke you up. Is Dusty coming?"

"Dusty's in Florida. You had a dream. There's nobody in your house. Drink some coffee."

The night Granny died, I'd been reading to her. I wish I could remember what book. It doesn't really matter. It might have been Henry James. Or Edith Wharton. I was teaching eleventh-grade English at the time. I'd been reading to her, then telling her about stuff happening at school, about Nora. She was mostly unresponsive.

"I'll be back tomorrow. Hang in there. You hang in there. I'll be back."

Every day before I left, I'd lay my head on the pillow next to her and tell her I'd be back. I drove to my mother's house that night, but I didn't get out of the car. I just turned around in the driveway and went back over to the hospital. I didn't think about what I was doing at all and parked in the loading zone. Visiting hours were over, but I just walked past the nurses' desk.

"I forgot something."

Granny was lying in bed, just like I left her.

"Listen, I... I think I've been wrong all along. I'm sorry. I've been saying the wrong things completely, and I want you to know that I am so sorry about all of that. It was just selfish. It's just... I'm going to miss you so much. Forever. But it has been enough. Everything you already did was enough, you understand? I will be okay. You can go now. I love you. Thank you. Goodbye."

I kissed her and I left. My mom was standing on the front porch when I got there, not fifteen minutes later. The hospital had already called. I didn't even get out of the car, just turned around in the driveway. They said she was gone before I made it out of the hospital. They had tried to catch me.

Chapter Twenty-Five

"For a man who rejected superstitions about death, he detailed with great specificity his intentions regarding the disposition of his remains. Chiefly, he requested burial in a plot adjacent to his mother's final resting place in a private cemetery in Queens, New York."

Reading about Houdini again. Granny's reports held up to be accurate in spirit, if flawed in some particulars. Since the first Weekly Reader biography, each account became increasingly nuanced and complex, deviating more and more from the romantic recollections she provided as the basis of my interest. I never could quite remember who brought him up first—me to her, or the other way around. I think I told her about the story in the Childcraft Encyclopedia volume, People to Know. The ones that stuck with me most were Lister, Schweitzer, Belle Starr and Houdini. The stories, respectively, involved being hit by a bus, falling out of a high window, being shot at, and nearly drowning.

My earliest memories are fire and water, and I'm never certain which was first. No adult in my life seems to remember either incident with any clarity, but both occurred while we lived in a house we left when I was three. I can prove that much through dates on the photographs, stamped in red by the Rabbit Photo Company.

My parents had taken me with them to a party at a nearby lake. I'd wandered off, out onto the pier, while the adults sat on the banks in those folding chairs with the crackly plastic woven strips drinking Pabst Blue Ribbon out of cans. That day was the first time I tasted beer. Shiny silver and cold.

I had on a new pair of white Keds. They made my feet look long and thin and grown-up. I liked how they felt on the wooden pier, the thumping noises they made when I ran. I noticed my shadow running alongside me on top of the water, and it looked tall and thin and grown-up, too. I jumped and skipped, watching my elegant shadow jump and skip with much more grace than my stout little girl frame. I'd never been particularly interested in looking at myself before. It had always been kind of anticlimactic. All of a sudden, I was freaking Narcissus. I couldn't get enough. Finally, I sat myself down on the pier and dangled my legs so that I could watch my shadow legs kick and spin like a ballerina's long, poetic limbs. My dainty shadow feet decorated with shadow bows that bobbed as I kicked. My real foot was close—it almost looked like the shadow foot. At the bottom of the arc, they nearly touched, like dancers meeting at center stage, like the sugar-plum fairies in the Nutcracker I had seen on TV on Christmas Eve. They needed to touch. That was part of the show, when they touched. I wasn't thinking about the pier anymore, just my feet, my shadow feet and legs, my slender grown self down there, and I needed to touch it, just with the edge of my toes—

And I fell. Everything turned sepia brown and dirty, the weeds climbing over me and covering me. And then I felt the soft hair of the bottom of the lake, up to my ankles, knees, I sank into the bed. The jolt I felt breaking the water was gone, the water was warm, and the light through the silt turned everything above my head to glittering gold. It was completely soundless. Then dark. And I thought I died, because I felt something tear me away, out of the earth I thought, like a radish, but it was just out of the lake.

She crouched over me, a slender woman with a dripping ponytail, until my mother grabbed me up and pushed my face into her shoulder and ran back to the bank where the rest of their friends and their coolers and grills were. I couldn't understand much of what she was saying—there were a lot of tears—but I heard her say to her friends "She had her watch on! She jumped in with her watch on!" For years I thought I lost a watch when I fell in the lake, until one day I realized I was three years old and didn't have a watch. I didn't jump in on purpose, either. It was the bystander who jumped in, and whose timepiece had concerned my mother so much.

I knew what she meant, even if she didn't.

One winter Houdini performed one of his famous stunts for a large crowd, even though the spot on the river where the performance was scheduled to occur had frozen over the night before. His managers and the event planners wanted to cancel the show, convinced that Houdini's safety would be compromised by these conditions. Houdini, however, was not one to disappoint a crowd. He performed his final show suffering a burst appendix: unwilling to cancel, he was revived between the first and second acts. Within a week he'd be dead, but that night the paying public saw his act completed.

Down he went then, under the ice. Once he freed himself from the chest in which he'd been tied and locked, Houdini found he'd drifted downstream from the hole in the ice where the trunk was dropped into the river. Out of breath and tired from completing the stunt itself, his outlet to fresh air was blocked solid by a sheet of ice. And here's the part that stuck in my kid brain, because it knocked me out that he figured this out blind, underwater. Maybe he'd read it someplace and remembered it. Maybe his DNA knew. Harry

Houdini understood the map of the human intuitively and completely; maybe he could connect to the behavior of nature as well, but something struck him and told him to find the tiny gap of air between the top of the moving river and the bottom of the frozen river, the slight wisp of air that existed in that hiatus. The illustration showed him in his antique swimwear, arced backwards, the flat of his nose pressed against the frozen sheet, his nostrils taking in just enough air to give him time to reorient himself and locate the rope his team had dropped through the ice hole. Enough time to swim to safety and emerge from the frozen lake a miracle, lost and retrieved, redeeming every witness on the shore who stood there praying for help, atoning for their sins, begging for a release from judgment this one time. He emerged, proof of a benevolent God.

Having fulfilled his obligation to his audience, Houdini went to his grave with a bundle of papers in his hands—letters from his mother, who left this earth while Houdini performed in Europe. She had asked him to bring her a gift from his trip, a pair of slippers. Safety and comfort. Houdini wrote to his brother in his grief, expressing his wonder at his own inability to let her go. Somehow, his design to travel into the afterlife was either meant to console his living self by holding the mental image of his physical possession of the letters after death, or the thought that the proper acts might reunite him with his beloved mother. The gnawing urge for what we can no longer hold in our hands. We can't help but grasp for it, even as the keepers of the sacred, the guards at the museum, watch us, hush us, tell us not to touch.

Houdini didn't believe the parlor frauds who came to him with news of his mother. Just like being able to find that slice of air under the ice, he could keep his head in the direst of disorienting circumstances. He could've been satisfied, partly, if he could've believed any of them, even a little. Instead, he built a rage within himself on behalf of all the desperately bereaved, even going so far as to argue to the United States Congress that fortune-telling and spiritualist fraud violated the concept of free speech in the manner of calling out "Fire!" in a crowded theater. They preyed on the suffering of others for financial gain, these charlatans. But personally, Houdini had another fear regarding the spiritualists. He worried that the poison of their deceit interrupted any real transmission of information from that other world. Rather than reuniting him with his heart, his lost mother, could it be that they were preventing her true messages from coming through?

Arthur Conan Doyle commiserated with Houdini about the scourge of the unimaginative, tacky crystal-ball gazers. In the course of their conversations, Houdini devised a plan to contact his wife from the other side, but definitively, with proof. Based on a code drawn from language in one of Conan Doyle's letters, Houdini gave his wife a specific message to expect from him, delivered only in the code they had invented. No other transmission would be accepted as legitimate. Granny, the least sentimental woman in the world, was completely charmed by this story—if Houdini couldn't prove the existence of an afterlife, he proved to my granny that a man could love enough in this world to be worth a damn. It was the best valentine, love poem, bunch of flowers, or candy heart ever delivered. A message in a code from Sherlock Holmes' creator. You can have your Romeo and Juliet, your Abelard and Heloise. He may have been the world's greatest magician, but to Granny, he was the world's greatest lover.

"Will you contact me?"

I'd ask her again, every time.

"What do you want me to say?" She'd laugh, then put the toothpick back in the side of her mouth.

"Well, if it's pretty over there..."

"Don't worry about it. Can't be any uglier."

"Isn't there anything in this world that you would miss? Don't you like... something? What about your cats?"

"Cats. They don't give a shit. They like the food. I don't like them either—I just can't stand to see anything suffer, is all. Or I wouldn't feed them. But if I don't, they just come around and cry and cry all day and night."

"What about... books?"

"I read the books to forget I'm here."

"Yeah." Me too. Back then especially.

"Nicky, I wouldn't miss anything. I'm ready for it to take me, whatever it is. The good Lord or the Devil. Or the big old hole. The only thing beautiful in this world to me is you."

There's not a whole lot to say to that. You see now why I didn't know what to do with those ashes. I had zero to work with.

Houdini's widow held séances every year on the anniversary of his death, conveniently October 31st. For ten years, she engaged the services of the leading psychics and mediums and spiritualists. The tenth year, the famous Mr. Ford called upon Harry Houdini to come forth, ring the bells, deliver his message. He called and called, with increasing urgency and flourish, until the resolute Mrs. Houdini called it off. "My last hope is gone," she said. "Ten years is long enough to wait for any man."

And she never attempted to reach him again.

Some reports say that Mr. Ford actually delivered the message that Houdini had given his wife to expect. She had been a stage actress in her day, and the message was a line from one of her favorite and most celebrated roles. I have to agree with Granny here: that's a real man right there. Houdini must have fallen in love with his wife on the stage, to make his soul's final message to her the repetition of her own words, a reflection of the image he loved. These were some lovely people.

Jonathan Safran Foer says art makes you say to someone, "I love this, you will love this." That the transmission of your own love for a work of art, when placed into the heart of another person, creates and perpetuates that love energy so that it never dies. This theory makes the giving of art—even the pointing out of something beautiful to a stranger—the deepest and most authentic act of love. Because even after you're gone, even if the object is gone, the love for it, the feeling it created, the admiration, the selflessness, the energy—it's still there. The Poodles brought it to us and brought us all to life. They left, but they left us this, this desire to show each other stuff. I love it. It's beautiful. It wasn't me, and it wasn't you, but now it's both of us because we touched it, and it entered our being. A house. A poem. A plant or a sunset. It's the jolt, the recognition. That part never dies. What did you hear, Mrs. Houdini, that October night? Or did you feel something low and prickly grabbing your wrist while you petted the cat's back?

A long time ago, we walked halfway home from a parents' meeting, Brad and me. Our friend Rich was home babysitting Nora. It was the first time we'd been in the same place alone for weeks. I'd been staying out all night, sometimes in the bookstore, sometimes at a bar. I'd walk home in the early morning, when the fishmongers and produce-stand people were just starting to hose down the bricks of the Pike Place Market. I'd come in and go to sleep, and he'd load the dishwasher over and over, go run errands while I played with Nora. Our life became incredibly stupid, for two smart people. I read a bunch of Oliver Sacks books. I drank. He drank more.

In a reflexive cinematic gesture, we had chosen to have it out, tepidly, on some overgrown steps to a vacant lot. Not a big-budget stereotype—more of an indie film full of New York actors like Hope Davis and Steve Buscemi. What a disappointment. We had much more of a Montgomery Clift/Elizabeth Taylor level of pathos and anger to vent. But instead I sat trying to keep away from empty Odwalla bottles and candy wrappers, condom packages and the stray needle or two. With peeling posters across the street for that TV show with Nicole Ritchie and Paris Hilton. The conversation was short, considering.

"You don't leave the house," I said. "You don't want to leave the house."

"I don't have to leave the house. I don't have to work."

"Everybody has to work."

"I don't have to work."

"I won't raise a child with no work ethic."

"Then she'll be from a broken home."

And that was it. There was one time I got mad—I think it was the last time I went inside our old apartment to get the last of my things. I managed to yell, out of context, "You broke my heart!" It was flat and anticlimactic.

Brad sold the apartment. We designed every inch of that thing, part Mackintosh, part Wright, everything built in with custom woodwork except the couch and our toothbrushes. Brad built a Mission-style box light fixture with milk-glass panels for the kitchen, big enough to hold a decent-sized goat. I ordered gilt rice paper from Japan for the upper border. The paint was dark, saturated Edward Gorey colors. Schoolhouse light fixtures. A tiny, hand-carved box built into the wall like a safe by the front door where we hung all our keys. It was a jewel box. It was the safest place I ever could have imagined. Some middle-aged Croc-wearing bitch bought it, pulled down the molding and painted everything beige. She'll go to hell for that.

Brad is still not answering. I can't leave a message about ashes. We'll have to get this straight another day.

I am fur-covered and soft-footed, I rise and fall, like the vapor of my breath. I beat the snow with my paws. At the crest of this hill I will leap and roll under the night sky. I will eat you so I can carry you with me.

Chapter Twenty-Six

It happened all at once. I was staring up at the fluted glass petals of the hall fixture. I'd been given some running cedar branches to drape around the entryway and over the sides of the pendant light, but I was thinking two things at once: that it would be a shame to cover up such a cool vintage piece, and that those branches would be a colossal fire hazard. That's when George found me.

They don't say anything—that's not how it happens. It starts like a fever, the way you feel a fever coming on. The memory comes later, if at all. What I get is how they felt in that moment, where I'm standing. Or close by. The really strong ones I'll dream about for years.

George didn't say anything when he dropped me to my knees in the apartment foyer that day. It was like falling in love. And having it end. All wrapped together in a ball of lightning I tried futilely to catch in my hands, and for a second I held the thing I wanted most in the world, but not long enough to name it and not hard enough to keep it.

Remember: all stories are love stories, and every alarm is a false one.

"I got one more bulb."

"Don't put it in your mouth. That doesn't seem like a good idea."

Vivian just winked at him as she climbed down a couple of rungs.

"I got to hold on with both hands. Hey, I used to sing that song with Louis Prima."

"I don't remember that song, Vivian."

"You're just too young, that's all. That one I'm not making up. 'Baby I ain't no rock-a Gibralta, gimme one look and I'm a-gonna falta."

"You sure you want to sing that on a ladder? Here—"

He held up the bowl for her to drop in the last dud, and he handed her the last fresh bulb.

"'You got hips like the shifting sands, ooh baby, I got to hold on with both hands!'"

"Vivian, don't dance on the ladder! Sheesh."

All that wiggling. George noticed the ladder feet had come off their marks and weren't aligned anymore, but they were nearly done with the task.

"Where were YOU when the lights went out—" She'd make that joke every time. Sometimes he'd try to remember. Where would I have been? Did they go out all at once? Maybe I was washing dishes when the first one went, George thought. Maybe I was at work, I was typing, for the second. Maybe they all went at once.

"The question, Vivian, is where were YOU when the lights went out? Your lights go out a lot, lady."

"Buddy boy, you have no idea. In my day. I got no lights left."

"You're brighter than most, Vivian."

"Pardon me if I take my time. This is the only screwing I do these days."

"Yeah, yeah. What about Mr. Abbot on the first floor?"

"That dried-up old prune? I'd rather kiss a gibbon's ass."

"That's a kink I've never heard before."

"Beggars can't be choosers. If beggars wished for horses, they'd all get an ass. Or something. Heh heh. The bartender at the Tower Bar used to give Rudy, my piano player—now he was a fancy man—he used to give Rudy a little shot a Galliano and say 'Here, Rudy, this'll put lead in your pencil.' And Rudy'd say 'Thanks, old sport, but I got no one to write to.'"

Vivian never married. There was a story George knew about a soldier. Maybe it was a soldier. Or a college man. Someone unavailable. And suddenly, it was forty years ago.

"Vivian! For God's sake. Were you into the sauce before I got here?"

"Hold on. I just got one more to screw. Said the debutante to her escort. Heh h—"

George, by all accounts, probably didn't even know what happened. But Vivian saw it all unfold, her loose slipper letting go of her heel, the ladder step sliding away. And then she was flying, airborne, and it was more thrilling than she could have imagined, almost like she was a radio wave or a stroke of heat lightning. It would've been the best way to go, she thought, except she couldn't help worrying about George underneath her—she tried to say Let Me Go! but nothing came out, and all she could hear was her heartbeat and his breath, one long deliberate gasp, as he sprung himself up to catch her. No, no! she tried to scream, but her mouth was held open in an Oh of shock, and that was all there could be. Just Oh. The light exploded, sparks showering them in a broken constellation. George never made another sound. Vivian could hear herself saying Sorry, Sorry, Sorry, No in her head, but it didn't come out, and he wasn't there to hear it.

The building manager found them like that, George holding Vivian's waist, Vivian's arms cast outward, her mouth still in that Oh of surprise. George's eyes were tightly shut, the fixture broken, the ladder overturned.

"Well," said the fireman to the manager, "It seems pretty clear what happened. What a shame, right?"

A wave of awkward feeling came over the building manager. It seemed to affect the fireman, too. Catching George and Vivian in what seemed to be an intimate scene of some kind. Of course, not lovers or anything, but... the manager looked around the foyer desperately.

"I guess being a fireman, you see it all," the manager said. "Maybe he thought he was her son?"

"Yeah, maybe. Still. What a way to start the week."

It's always starting, life, all of our lives, about to start, beginning every day again until that one day the world's round mouth opens and says "over" and "over" and "over."

The stories, the souls, they remind me of each other, all of them. Enough so that sometimes I wonder if they are the ones who recognize it in me, the shape of the same holes in all of our hearts. But then, is that hole there all your life? I don't believe in predestination. I do believe some of us are magnetized by love. I believe that not all attractions are positive. What kind of permittivity is that?

Driving on the interstate to work, I pass a couple of decent-looking hotels, a Westin and a Sheraton maybe, and sometimes I think that might be a nice place to take a bunch of heroin and die. I've never been suicidal, but sometimes a nap didn't seem like enough of a pause to lift the bag of cement off of my brain. Put on some headphones, Joy Division or Brian Eno. Lie down on the floor. Like I used to do on the shellacked orange wooden floor in my first apartment, only for real this time. Never making it to the Modern English concert that night in Raleigh in 1986, never meeting my ex-husbands, never meeting my lost son.

Then later, on the floor of the empty apartment next door in Atlanta. That party in about 1990. Everybody's hair was really, really long on at least one side. You couldn't see anybody's face, and everybody was stretched out on the floor, like the REM video where everybody falls down. Black coats, plaid flannel and hair, and everybody falling down. Amy's brother was facing me, a few feet away, and I remembered the tequila bottle sliding over, his arm sticking out of the trench coat to push it spiraling my way. Everybody fell down that night.

Floors I have known. Curled up on the stair landing of a modern condo with pale hardwoods, a boy leaning against the railing asleep. I can't even remember which city that was, which year. Then the night the doorman from the ReBar was holding my head up from the soft shaggy rug with hypnotic patterns in the old house on Capitol Hill in Seattle. "I'm doing a card trick," he kept saying, "and you can't see it if you're on the floor like that." Waking up in the sun on the warm boards of a dock on Puget Sound. Dressed in Victorian undergarments, provided by the hostess? One of the actors from the show the night before, swinging in the hammock, in a kimono.

When I was little, I'd get scared late at night after the day's programming ended and the national anthem finished to white noise. I'd curl up on the blue plush shower rug in my parents' bathroom, a bright white cell with all the lights on. It still felt like the thing was in there, crouching on the shower bench, squinting and crackling. Eyes wide, I'd stare at the octagonal tiles, trying to connect the random blue octagons scattered among the white ones with as few grout lines as possible until the window turned light blue with distant sunlight.

Down on the ground, it always gets to that point. On the dock next to a battleship, refusing to get up because I was too scared to look at it. On the cemetery path, trying to go forward at a crawl while a voice I didn't know seemed to have me by the ankles, begging me to leave it alone. Late at night in the lonely bright box in the tobacco field. I wanted to lie down on the ground, all those times. I wanted to lie down in the lightning fields. That's what I want to hear from them all. When will I lie down in the lightning field?

"Come quick! I think Nicole fell off the ladder!" But I hadn't fallen, exactly. Not like they thought. It was all I could do to tell them I was alright, because I was mostly, even if I was at a loss to explain to them why I couldn't take my eyes off the lights overhead. What could I tell them? I had no intention of ruining a perfectly good Christmas party.

"Are you sick? You're not pregnant, are you?"

"She might be dehydrated."

"Get her some water! Honey, you have got to start taking better care of yourself."

When you look up, what do you see? Is it cold where you are? I can feel it in my teeth, but I'm not sure when I bite down—if it's the cold that I feel. What I need to hear is not a song. Where are your eyes? Sometimes, I'm almost certain that it really is you right beside me.

Voice, who are you really? How do I reach you when the sled won't stop, when it just keeps taking you farther from me?

CHAPTER TWENTY-SEVEN

"THEY HOPPING OFF. LOOK."

"Still on one foot?"

"Yep."

"It's pretty strange, isn't it."

"Yep."

"Are they gonna be okay?"

"Nope."

"Well. That's no good. Can we help them?"

"Noooope."

It was a definitive nope—it came with a slow headshake.

"Okay then. Can we go to the living room? Think that's okay?"

"Yeah, it's okay. They went away."

Down at the bottom step, Edgar leaned out and peered off to the right for a few seconds. Then he looked back at me and smiled.

"Come on," he said. "I got to fix in the living room. I need my tools."

And so the Hopping-on-One-Foot tribe joined Jesus and the Cubble, the lady in the chair, the man in the boat in the backyard, and the people who wave at us from the edge of the woods. And Alice, and Miss Beverly. Lord knows. Don't forget Miss Beverly.

I had been describing my day with Edgar to Thomas. I

can't help but feel responsible somehow, but Thomas doesn't seem terribly upset.

"Who could forget Miss Beverly. Hopping on one foot? I don't suppose he gave any other details." Thomas folded his hands across the back of his head and exhaled. It's a gesture I've come to recognize. It's funny, but it turns out that's exactly what unconditional acceptance looks like.

"Not really. Only that they're gone, and we can't help them."

"That's just great. Not creepy at all. Have they been back?"

"If they have, I haven't heard about it."

"Ha. Okay then."

Thomas seemed content to let the whole narrative stand on its own, especially since we had other concerns at the moment. With all the plastic sheeting spread out, it sure looked like we were up to no good. The kids were both at my mom's. We had the evening open to get this worked out, but the time had come.

"Are you ready to do this? I know we've got a plan, but if you are the least bit uncomfortable, now would be the time..."

"No, this is it. There's not going to be a better opportunity. Let's make it happen, cap'n."

Thomas brought the axe up, but I screamed like a little girl.

"I'm sorry, I'm sorry—I'm okay."

"I can still back this whole thing up—"

"No—it was just—that was catharsis, not terror—"

"We talked about this. It's liable to be a little hard. You don't know what exactly it's going to look like. No way to know. You ready?"

"Yep. You go. Go on ahead. Thanks."

"You sure?"

"I'm good."

"We could have somebody else do it."

"Nope. Too much paperwork. Too much of a trail. This way, nobody knows anything."

"All right."

He swung, and it was over quickly. The wooden box just flew into bits, in kind of a surprise reaction.

"Okay, that was easy. But we knew the next part would be the hardest. I'm going to need the blowtorch now."

"Yeah. I sort of feel like I didn't get my money's worth from the crematorium. What kind of wood was that, anyway? It's like it was the Ikea urn. Here. Here's the cord, too."

"Still okay?" Thomas puts a steady hand on my shoulder.

"Oh yeah. Let's finish it now. Let's go while the momentum's on our side."

Human remains. It's not like the movies where everything works out elegantly and with dignity. But with the plastic sheeting we caught all the powdery ash that escaped the metal urn liner once we unsealed it—more like destroyed it. We put everything in a shoebox, the only one I could find at Mom's. It was leopard print and hot pink.

"Well, you do wear her leopard coat."

I did. It came from Ellisburg's in Cameron Village in about 1968, and she wore it anyplace important or fun that we ever went when I was a little kid. She used to say it was real, but of course it's not real leopard, and anyone can see so. Maybe she just meant it wasn't a figment of your imagination.

"I don't know. It seems unrelated."

"So, it's an ugly shoe box. You'd rather use a Trader Joe's bag? I'm running out of options here."

"The shoebox is fine. It's like taking the subway to the Met—whatever. You still hear the opera the same as the ones who came in a carriage."

"I have no idea about any of that. But if it helps you feel better, then yes." Thomas is ever practical. I don't know what I'd do if it were any other way.

We shook the loose bits into the shoebox like the last dregs of flour into cake batter. Thomas duct taped it up, and I sat it on my lap in the truck, just like I had on the airplane when I moved out west and brought her with me. I'd been kind of fresh with her on that trip. I gave her a hard time about not traveling with me when she was still alive. This time, I had different things to say.

"I'm sorry about this hideous box. It's inappropriate. But not as inappropriate as the Duchess of York photographed in a bikini while pregnant. Not as inappropriate as Bella Abzug's hats. Not as inappropriate as the manager of the Piggly Wiggly, who made you cry when he moved the cat food aisle three times in a six-month period. It's an indignity, and it's my fault—this resulted from my poor planning. But I hope the necessity of expediency and the superiority of the end result will allow you to forgive this temporary shame."

"Cat food aisle. I don't think I heard—"

"I'll explain later. Granny, Thomas—you know Thomas; you've been living in his house—Thomas is helping me with a plan that I think you'll be happy with. Here's the thing: I know Willie and Alice are waiting for you. I know my grandfather is waiting for you."

I stopped. So far, that list included only people she'd like.

"Ruth is waiting for you."

That's okay, I thought. She missed Ruth.

"Henry Kissinger is waiting for you."

"Nic..."

"He is. You can tell him all about—"

"Nic, Henry Kissinger is not dead."

"What? You're kidding. He's 175 years old. He was 175 years old when I was ten."

"No, you were ten, and fifty looked like 175. He's very much alive. Google confirms it."

"Granny, Henry Kissinger is on the way. Any time now—you be on the lookout. He might be disoriented—that'll be your chance. Dean Martin is waiting for you—"

I glanced at Thomas.

"Oh, you're good there," he said. "I'm pretty sure."

"And Rudolph Valentino, and Bob Hope. And you can go kick Frank Sinatra and Richard Nixon's asses."

"Twice for me on the Nixon. Please."

"Oh, and, and, fucking Jane Austen! I mean, go find Jane

Austen, and Dickens, and Wilkie Collins! Go find Emily
Brontë! Oh, man go find Ella Wheeler Wilcox and the Casa-
bianca lady that Whitman liked, she had three names, too…
Selicia Dorothea… something…".

I was getting a little off course, but it seemed right.

"And Longfellow. You guys can recite *Hiawatha* for fucking
all eternity together. You can teach him 'Running Bear Loved
Little White Dove' and 'Kaw-liga,' since those all kind of go
together for you in some hugely politically incorrect way, but
whatever. Do *Evangeline,* too, because it's pretty. And tell him I
like 'Chaucer,' with all that internal, boxy imagery…"

"This could get long. You realize."

"So the point I'm making by bringing all this up, Granny,
is that I think you'll like our plan."

I liked our plan. And there was still part of me that
thought that all of this trouble had been self-imposed, that
there were no disruptions outside of my own anxiety. That
our rage for unconventionality, mine and hers combined,
had robbed us both of the common relief that our shared
culture gives us all. If I had gone along with Mom's idea and
had a regular funeral, I probably would never have given it
another thought. And if I had, I would've had the best built-
in excuse in the world: it's not what I wanted, but nobody
would let me do what I wanted.

We were doing exactly what I wanted. It felt like a lot of
responsibility. Most days I spent eating popcorn, watching the
parade. Once in a while, I felt like the glove on the hand of a
beauty queen, waving at the crowd. Today, today turning into
tonight—I was a full-on float, a motherfucking Bullwinkle
balloon, loosed from its tether and taking my crazy on the

road. Fuck the parade. I'm Bullwinkle, and I AM the parade.

We got to the construction site at the gray part of day that thinks it's not its job to watch what's going on exactly. From a distance, everything looks passable. We weren't dressed like ninjas, all in black. Just our work clothes. I'd changed out of my skirt into some jeans. But we were average-height people in blue-and-white clothes. Maybe gray and white. In a gray midsized vehicle with in-state plates too far away to read. We moved slowly, but not too slowly. And not tentatively. We did have a leopard-print shoebox that distracted from our faces.

"According to these plans, the entry is over here, and that way would be the auditorium and the hall with the offices, the restrooms—"

"Plan B."

"I don't think Plan B will be necessary. If we just walk around that corner over there, we're on the back side, where the picture windows will be."

"The shelves will be a few feet in, out of the direct sunlight."

"Is that your phone? Are you answering your phone right now?"

"It's Francis! That's fucking amazing. Hold on, hold on. I've been trying to—hey—Hey! Francis. Oh my God. You won't believe where I am."

"I don't think he'll have a problem believing."

"So, so, so—yes, that blur in the photo WAS the mist. But I think it's gone. I did try that, with the hairbrush. I asked nicely. Perpendicular to where I left it. Perfectly. I'm sure. I think so."

Thomas was smoking a cigarette and keeping an eye on the cars moving in and out of the Bed Bath and Beyond parking lot across the road.

"So I have her ashes in a shoebox and I'm standing right where the new library is getting built. They're pouring the foundation tomorrow."

There's a time and a place for technology. I think my concept of what either of those might be expands a little every day. Probably according to expediency and my own self-ish needs in most cases. But every once in a while, there is elegance in the expanding universe.

The speaker wasn't very loud, and Francis's face was rather small, but it was just us and we were all close together: me and Thomas in our bodies, Francis and Granny in spirit. One assisted by current technology and propped up on a cinder-block, the other assisted by the technology of our hearts, the hunger in our being to say the things we couldn't before, to do the things that we couldn't imagine, the things that seemed beyond our power. Until those things became essential.

"Ready, Francis?"

"Darling, I'm right here."

"Remind me later to tell you about Edgar's encounter with the Hopping-on-One-Foot people."

"Later!" Thomas and Francis both said.

Later, in the car on the way back, I told Thomas I wished there'd been a big electrical storm right then. With lightning crashing.

"It was not enough that the ungrounded wires were over there quacking like a herd of ducks?" Thomas had asked.

"I don't think you call ducks a 'herd.'"

"I think anything you call them, other than 'quack,' is pretty arbitrary."

It was a valid point.

In the moment, I didn't even notice the power lines or posts. I did hear Thomas muttering about what a mess the site was, but Thomas is particular about that kind of thing, having built like thirty houses when he was working for Habitat for Humanity. Plus I just thought he was having a "your-tax-dollars-at-work" moment.

"I hope they fix this shitty wiring so they don't burn the place down once it's full of books."

That's right—he did say that. Because I said, "What's permanent? Nothing. The wise men's eyes will still be glittering when the hunk of rock they are carved into is dust. That's the only thing that lasts. The glittering. The spark."

I didn't say that, but I was thinking it, or something like that, if not ordered so well or as clear. I was feeling it. And I was muttering something like, "Now would be a good time for some lightning," when Thomas called over.

"You're right there. According to the papers."

"According to the papers, Granny, this is where you go back to what you love most." Thomas had the camera raised. Taking a picture, a last-minute addition to the plan about which I was still not sure. But it was my one chance.

"Wouldn't it be perfect if she ended up under the Brontës?"

"We're long past perfect."

And then there was a little flash.

Meaning, we were all still there. It wasn't lightning, just the camera. Just the expected. Everything went as planned.

I tried to remember everything Thomas told me about how a semiconductor works. The PN junction—it allows the flow of the electrons in one direction, but not the other. There was a whole lot of electric potential out here amid the sand and wires, the dark sky like a question. No, like an answer for a question waiting to be asked. Francis still there on my phone, in my hand. I had to think: were the soles of my shoes rubber? How dense was I in electrons? How thin was my grasp of this concept? Is there such a thing as Romanticism in engineering? There ought to be. Semiconductor—that's a poor level of commitment. Where's the Megaconductor? I want completeness. I want something to be whole. To be finished. Where is my magic?

"I don't want to be a semiconductor!"

"Well great! Then let's get in the truck and get out of here."

"No! I mean... is that lightning? Can you explain permittivity to me again, one more time? Because the lightning, if it would strike right here—"

"Nic, will you stop for a minute? What is this? Are you trying to make some kind of wormhole to crawl through? Do you need to shake hands with her or something? Enough. It's enough already. Isn't it? How far did you really want this to go?"

This wasn't the longing for some lost past. It wasn't some stranger's sadness. It was me, and it was Thomas. Right here and now. It was potential—electric potential, the question: Are you leaving now? Are you going away now? Even in your mind, are you moving away from me while we stand here? What are you choosing right now—me or the picture of something else? Because I was *doing*, not listening, for once. The next thing to happen was not going to be something that had happened already. Not if I could shake myself loose from other peoples' stories long enough to go back to writing my own.

The rain was going to start now, any minute. Thomas stood there, the truck door open, leaning toward me, his face lit a little by the radio display.

"Nic, don't you believe in anything?"

He was asking me that. Not the other way around. I had to think.

"Thomas?"

"What now?"

"Is it okay if I drive? Home?"

Chapter Twenty-Eight

I HAD TO ADJUST THE SEAT as far up as it would go, move all the mirrors. I sat still for a minute after starting the engine, Thomas coming around the other side of the truck while the wind picked up and the rain began in seriousness. He stubbed out the last bit of a cigarette and tore up the filter before climbing in.

"I want to be buried in the Lightning Field."

"Okay. Are we talking about an actual place? In the known world?"

"It's an art installation out west someplace."

"Of course. Don't worry. I'll find it. When the time comes, I'll just GPS it."

"Scattered, actually. Not buried."

"Of course."

Months later, when the library was all finished, I thought about going to the dedication. They had a ribbon cutting, and somebody from the history department at UNC Wilmington was going to speak about the pottery exhibit that would be the inaugural feature display and lecture series. But it wasn't about me now. It wasn't about her, either, but I like to imagine her listening to them over in the auditorium, remembering her pale blue Fiestaware cup, touching the ridges on its sides with her fingers.

I did go to the library, finally, maybe six months or a year later. It was hard to tell exactly, once the building was there, but when I saw the power line poles out the picture window, I got oriented pretty quickly. I looked at the shelves. IRS publications. Tax Law for Dummies. Income Allowance: Maximize Your Refund.

Death and Taxes.

Francis's voice came back to me. I'd had enough trouble saying the Lord's Prayer when months back I'd had to light the Agua Florida on my front porch steps, even if I was reading it off my phone screen. I almost set fire to one of the pencil firs, flailing around with that giant match. There was no way I could think of anything good to say while I was spreading her ashes on the ground so they could be covered in concrete the next morning. I'd already pronounced Henry Kissinger dead and wished aloud to be struck by lightning. Gratitude filled my heart as I listened to Francis, glancing over from time to time to see Thomas's reassuring expression and Francis's tiny face hovering on the screen. It was like having a pocket wizard. Francis would be a great app, I thought. In a series of inappropriate thoughts I was having that evening, that was one of them.

"Let the Earth absorb our departed sister," Francis said, "and let her spirit find peace in this place of understanding, acceptance and wisdom. And let us find consolation as we move forward through this world until the day that our energies meet again on another plane. Let only good spirits guide us and visit us from this moment forward. Admit to our sphere only the energies of the Light, and let us find strength in their presence and love. Let the darkness take back the dark and heal it. Let us seek no more after what is lost to us. Let us grieve no more."

Chapter Twenty-Nine

I can't leave them undone, and the girls won't leave me. I knew their story from the time I met Addie under the arbor. It was only filling in. Filling in and fact-checking. But there's only one place it could go...

"You can't go in, Addie. She's very contagious at this stage. There's nothing you can do for her, anyway. It won't be long."

Addie had stopped talking. Dr. Kron, exhausted from caring for one ill daughter and worried for his older child, could not conceal his consternation. But he had to find something to distract her so that she would not enter the sick room against his wishes.

"Addie! The best thing you can do for her—do you still have the eucalyptus you were growing? Go out to the greenhouse and find me some of that eucalyptus—"

Addie could only stare blankly at him and nod, her face contorted in pain. She ran out the front door, her coattails flying. Dr. Kron had seen this kind of thing before, in a patient from Baden. Usually hysteria is temporary, brought on by extreme circumstances. As these were. But Addie's energy and awareness were so much brighter, animated—his other patient had been an abject screamer, but with no industry, not like Addie's manic cleaning, cooking, sewing. Riding the poor horse into a lather, up and down the mountain. Lizzie was not going to recover, but Dr. Kron prepared himself for the fact that he might be grieving two daughters if he couldn't bring Addie back from her despair.

Back in the bedroom, Lizzie's breathing had flattened to

a rasp. She hadn't spoken in days. She was gone. The flu this year was a different one, a terrible respiratory infection set in with many of his patients. Anyone already susceptible had little chance. Lizzie had been sickly as a child, always wheezing, the fragile lungs of a baby born prematurely. Dr. Kron felt that the outdoors had helped her, that she had outgrown her childhood issues. But at the onset of her illness, he saw her weaken, then break, all of the old frailties returning, amplified.

Addie frantically shuffled through the bottles in every cabinet and shelf of the greenhouse.

"Move, cat. Get!"

The eucalyptus plant itself was down to nothing, but there were clippings somewhere; she'd saved some, dried them—surely they hadn't used them all. She gathered some other herbs together—her father might object on scientific grounds, but they must try everything—the old books could be right about things science doesn't yet understand. She had seen it before, that old woman in Baden. Nothing could stop the malaise that had stricken the young girl until she showed up with her case of jars. Addie had been to see her a few times since.

He wouldn't listen, and she knew it. She hid the bottles in her apron pocket. He couldn't stay in the room all night.

When Addie went to leave the greenhouse, she threw open the door—and jumped back in terror, knocking a shelf of bottles to the ground with a crash that sent the cat scurrying loudly and angrily through her skirts and out into the arbor. There he was, her father, right at the threshold.

"I didn't mean to startle you."

"Oh God—is she—"

"No—not yet, no. I'm sorry—I should have realized you'd think—I'm sorry, but I haven't heard you speak in days—"

Dr. Kron removed his eyeglasses. He had started to weep as he spoke, and he was too tired and too frightened to be embarrassed about it in front of his daughter.

"Father. Daddy." Addie sank down to her knees, sobbing. Dr. Kron lifted her back up.

"You can't. You can't leave me, too, Addie. I need you here with me. Lizzie is dying, and while we can't save her, we can help her pass in peace and without pain. Do you understand what I am saying? You don't have anything in those pockets of yours that will bring your sister back to you. The fever has taken her wits, and in a few more hours it will take her breath. I need you to be in this place right now, Addie. Here."

Addie hung her head and would not meet his gaze. Her sorrow convulsed her. Limp, pale, wet and shaking, she howled in pain.

"Addie, when your mother died, I felt this. Your head won't let you believe what is happening. It's telling you if you can take yourself away, if you can imagine another place to be, that this pain will leave you. That this won't be happening. It's not true, though, and your poor heart knows it isn't. Do not leave me, Addie! Though I know it seems cruel to ask you to do this, I need you to stand up and tell me you will not leave this place—not even in your head."

Addie straightened a little and looked at her father's face, because she had never heard him talk to her so urgently before. He was always direct, prescriptive, and clear, but she'd never heard the underlying tone she was hearing now. She heard doubt. She'd never known her father to doubt anything. And he was doubting her, right now. She had failed him, just for a moment. And it had thrown everything out of order.

"I will never leave this place. I swear it."

This is why they stay here. This is how the stories cling to us like static.

♭

It feels like I've been running forever. My heart is breaking. There is nothing left of me but ice, and it's breaking apart.

CHAPTER THIRTY

"FRANK SINATRA WAS A SON OF A BITCH," Granny said. "He wouldn't have been nothing without the Mafia. I saw the skinny bastard at that dinner table, and he was happy enough to know them then. You gotta dance with who brung you."

"You met Frank Sinatra?"

"Sure. At least he was better than that Frankie Valli kid. Thug. Tony had to go bail him outta jail all the time. His mother would call, crying, 'My baby, they got my baby in the jailhouse!' Off he'd go again to get Valli's sorry ass out and send him home to his mama. Be back in again in a few days, the thief. He was a little shit. A disrespectful little shit. I liked Louis Prima. Now, there was a man."

It was New Year's Eve, so we were watching Guy Lombardo. For Granny, it had to be a little depressing. She used to see him in person in New York. Now every year she sat out in the middle of a tobacco field with a fat little hillbilly Girl Scout who was full of questions and speculation. We toasted every few minutes with plastic champagne glasses full of Collins mixer I'd stolen out of my parents' bar. I think we blew on the same old noisemakers that said Welcome 1968 for about ten years. She had a silver tiara with white crepe paper, and I had something like a drum major's hat in a metallic pink.

"Lady of Spain, I adore you. Pull down your pants—I'll explore you."

Granny didn't think much of an accordion. But she liked the waltzes, like the next piece. The ladies in this number all had glittering gold skirts that fanned out like twirling suns. The men held the ladies' hands high so they could spin about.

"I'm going to have four children, two boys and two girls. Then when they grow up, they can marry each other."

I was probably only five or six years old. Still, I'm not sure where I dug up that idea.

"Brothers and sisters cannot marry each other, first of all." Granny lit up another Bel Air. "And second, four young 'uns. You'd have to shoot me. Jesus H. Christ. Shoot me. While I jump off a bridge."

About 11 p.m., she'd crack open another beer.

I called her every year for the countdown to midnight. New Year's Eve 1989, I was weaving through the crowd to the ladies' room at the Euclid Avenue Yacht Club—I got desperate and walked part of the way on the bar, finally emerging with about a minute and a half of the Eighties yet left. That's about all anybody ought to take of the Eighties. About halfway through "We Built this City" is all you can stand. Anyway, my friends who were standing on the booth table in the front window were waving like shipwrecks at me. I asked for the bar phone.

"Hey!"

"Hey!"

"Who is this?"

"It's me, Granny. Happy New Year! Ten years ago we were watching the Village People singing 'Ready for the Eighties' on the TV right now!"

"I can't understand you."

Valid.

"Happy New Year!"

"Oh. You too!"

"I'm in a bar!"

"I'm in Raleigh. At the house."

"I know! I called you there!"

"Thank you. Go back to your party. Happy New Year. I'll talk to you later."

She hung up. She'd do that. It was part of the deal with a phone conversation with her. All phone calls with her were basically proof-of-life situations.

She's been set to rest now. I'm sorry I'm not doing anything about your ashes yet. What I am most sorry about is that you didn't get to tell this story to anybody else but me. I'm your only audience member. Like the Language poets—they've got nobody but me, and I worry that I've been pretty poor support. I was there for that one big reading at that one MLA conference in Philadelphia. The one where everybody in the whole room read poems, except for me. I was the one true audience member, the one with no separate voice, no plan, no agenda. I got there, picked up a program, found a seat. There were about twenty names listed for readers on the front of the program. I turned it over, and there looked to be about twenty more names. In all, there were thirty-seven readers and an emcee who read as well. I started looking at the room, counting the four or five people around the snacks and drinks, the ten or so sitting and staring at their stacks of papers. The two dudes struggling with a PA. There were a couple of billowy teens installing some kind of top-heavy papier mâché waterfowl on the back wall, but they turned out to be on a different mission altogether and were gone before the poems began. I was number thirty-nine in the room.

I was celebrated like a Mayan sacrifice. Like a unicorn. The thing about Language poetry—well, years later, on one of our early dates, I had taken Thomas along with me to a local reading. I recognized some names in the list of one of the presenter's influences, and as he ascended the podium, I grabbed Thomas's arm gently, fixed him with my gaze and said, "Don't panic. It will be over soon." Later he thanked me for giving him something to grasp while he wondered whether he'd suffered a stroke, and whether his cognitive functions would return. After the MLA reading that night in Philadelphia, and the delivery of what must have been at least thirty-eight distinct poems, the assembly adjourned to a pub and invited me along. Charles Bernstein bought me drinks. "I just finished a dissertation on Laura Riding," I said. "I quoted you." Many, many words issued forth from both of us. I mentioned geometry, time, space, mirrors, the possibility of synonyms, the color white, trajectories, electricity, Barrett Watten—

"Oh, he's right over there," Charles said. "You should tell him! He would be fascinated to know that you integrated so much of that book into your argument."

But one unicorn is reluctant to approach another. I was the single audience member, I was the center of all Language poetry. And all of Language poetry was crowded around a wooden wagon wheel heavy with craft beer. Even when pressed together, all we could do was smile awkwardly at one another while mourning the nature of our exchange, bounded as it was by time, space, Colonial memorabilia and beverages. If only we were on a blank geometric plane. With a thesaurus.

At one point, after a few whiskies, I did manage to convey to the politely curious Charles Bernstein that I held every confidence that they would not find much to admire in my work.

"It's not like what you all do. Oh, no. I'm afraid mine is full of bric-a-brac."

It was one glorious evening in Philadelphia.

Come to think of it, if you had to be born and only have one audience member, I'm not such a bad one to be it. I don't know who picked me to be your mother, but I can't criticize the choice. The fact that I talk a lot, for instance. Maybe that's important. I haven't talked as much about you yet—maybe for some of the same reasons I don't talk to people about Language poetry. Talking about death doesn't always go well, and talking about the death of a child... I can do it, but I have to prepare people first—otherwise, it's really overwhelming for them. One of the most beautiful things about life is how many people can go through it without having anything truly awful happen. Except for dying at the end, and even that seems like sometimes it's not so bad. And anyway, we don't know, so if you play your cards right, this whole trip can be a cakewalk.

Of course, that's the view from over here. It's easy for living people to go around saying, "Thank goodness he's at peace now" or "Free at last!" or "He lived a full life," or the dreaded "It was God's will." Somebody actually said to me that you were too good for this world. That was butt-stupid. You would've done great here—what a freaking tough soul you were.

You helped me—remember the ultrasound, with the two doctors, and the one looked like George Clooney, and the whole thing was so sketchy they each sat by one of my ears and talked into it the whole time because they couldn't let

me lose consciousness but I had to be almost dead weight for
them to do the procedure? And we could see you the whole
time. Since they were anesthesiologists, and the ultrasound
doctors were busy doing their thing with the array of needles
and screens and tubes, they couldn't figure out at first what
was what with you. But I told them where to look to find your
head. "Over there, the top left, just below the numbers—
that's his elbow."

They guessed I must have seen you a lot on those screens,
that I had become an expert in locating your body parts. That
was true. I realized I had accomplished that, at least. I did
know you, I could recognize your silhouette by then. Your
round cheeks. They kept talking, one in one ear, the other in
the other, round and round like that Yoko Ono sound spinning around my head in the headphones. I was on Jupiter
that day, but I still knew what was going on.

It almost seemed like you were looking back at us, the
fourth person in a transmitted conversation, headphones
and wires, convoluted and disconnected sometimes. A weird
Language poem. You wouldn't have been a Language poet;
you had a sullen pride like your sister. The one word I asked
for both of you (because I repeated it for her, even after what
happened with you), was Fearless. You were fearless. Even if
you were angry.

Nobody likes to be interrupted, and you and I were interrupted. We were just starting a conversation. It's going to
continue. It may have been continued from before. I didn't
get a chance to do much, to do much of anything right, except for the one and only thing that mattered, at least during
this part of the conversation. These ashes are not nothing,
but they are like the image of you on the screen, the shadow

of you that I could recognize, that could hear me, my voice, the voices in my left ear and my right ear, talking about what a miracle you were, what a miracle you are, to have existed as long as you did.

CHAPTER THIRTY-ONE

ONCE YOU CAN LET THEM GO, once you can listen without your own desire, you realize they are everywhere, like electricity. Their stories run across the world under us all every day, under our feet, under our eyelids. All you have to do is listen...

"Addie? Are you awake?"

"Lizzie? Where are you? How did you get all the way over here?"

"I couldn't sleep so I came to see you."

"It's the middle of the night. We'll both be ruined tomorrow. Take this blanket—you'll freeze. Were you outside? In the damp air?"

"I bounded. I didn't touch the wet grass, don't worry. I covered my hair with my shawl." Lizzie giggled at Addie's superstition—like their mother, she insisted that wet hair could make you catch cold.

Addie had folded up her legs so Lizzy could curl up on the other end of the bed. They faced each other cross-legged, like they might start to sing out to a playmate and her dollies three.

"It was lovely tonight," Lizzie said.

"Running in the wet grass under the moon, like a wild animal?"

"No, silly. The music. Don't you wish you could hear more, more, more? I want my life to be like that. A soiree, with punch and dancing and gowns, and lovely people."

Addie thought for a minute. "You can have that, Lizzie. That's a fine life for you."

"Don't you want that life, too, Addie? Why can't we both do that? I don't want it to be my life—I want it to be our life."

"I'm happy to go back to the mountain, to help Father. He'll expect that, you know. I'm happy there—I have my work, my greenhouse."

"You have your friends in Baden. Those ladies. Do they teach you how to make potions with your flowers, Addie?"

"The point is, I don't mind it. I always feel a little out of place in a parlor full of—"

"But Addie, I won't go without you. I can't!"

"You don't understand, Lizzie. Father didn't want to burden you, but the problems with Mother's family... he doesn't have the money to pay for our tuitions here anymore. We're going home after this term. But maybe you can stay—I can talk to him—"

"NO! Addie, no—I won't. I won't stay without you!"

"Hush! You will wake this whole hall, and then what? Look, Lizzie—the mountain is no place for you. You belong in those parlors. You know how to talk to those people, and they love you. You come to life there. But the only way—"

Addie heard a little shuffling and saw a light briefly under the door, then it moved along.

"...the only way for you to live in Raleigh," she continued, "or in New York maybe one day, or even Paris—Lizzie, you find one of those lovely families with a nice son you can tolerate, and they will take care of you. You can write poems, order your dresses from Fauteuil's..."

"You shush. Daddy hasn't said a word to me about coming home. He wouldn't do that. We're learning, we are working diligently as we promised! He won't break his promise to us."

"It won't be his fault—it's that dreadful brother of Mother's. I won't call him Uncle."

"Addie, you always love to fuss about grown-up worries. It'll come to nothing. You'll see. I've been writing to him and he has said nothing, nothing, nothing about having to leave St. Mary's."

"Still. Make the most of your time here, Lizzie. It's your way to the life you want. This is your chance. You should go. Do not try to take me with you. The mountain is my home, and I'm happy to stay there."

They heard steps in the hall, and the light crept in under the door, reaching further into their safe chamber.

Lizzie slid out the window before Addie could stop her.

"Adele! Why aren't you in bed? Are you ill?"

"Not at all, Madame. It's the moon. The light was so bright it woke me, and I came to the window to close these drapes. I regret if I have disturbed you—please accept my apology."

"No matter. Some girls are awake on this hall—have you heard them? I've been up and down these halls all night, and I just can't seem to find where they've gone."

The clunk and blast of the old central air unit brings me back to the library table, the pencil, the magnifying glass in my hand. When I shudder free, I'm certain I've been staring at this page of her journal for hours, maybe. Rose varieties. I'm drowsy from deciphering schoolhouse script, rudimentary French. All I want is for it to be time to go down to the Crunkleton for a rye, preferably something I've never heard of before.

↯

They sleep, standing in their harnesses. I can see their thoughts and their tongues. They're hungry, they say. They say it's almost morning.

CHAPTER THIRTY-TWO

NORA TAKES OUT her penguin-shaped ear buds and stares at me until I stare back.

"So can I tell you about this dream I've been having? I'm looking at my iPod, going through my music. And it keeps playing, but it's not my music—I don't recognize it. Even if I have headphones on it keeps playing from speakers I can't find, it keeps downloading more of this music and it's terrible, it's full of swear words, and loud, and I can't get it to stop. There's more and more and more, and people keep looking around. Why are you laughing?"

"Wonder what that's about."

"I do. I mean, do you know what it is? What is it? What's it mean?"

"Do you have the dream about going into the bathroom, and then it's a giant bathroom, and you finally find a stall door and you go in, but then once you sit down you realize there are no walls? And you can see people walking around and stuff?"

"No—wait, yes—I think I've had a dream where the bathroom walls fall down."

"I have it about once a week. Half the time it turns out I'm in the men's room. They don't seem to notice me at least."

"Yeah. Or a huge bathroom, but all the stalls are broken or don't have doors. But this one is the same every time—this really loud music, and my headphones are plugged in but it's still just blasting out everywhere..."

"See? It's your creativity, your—whatever you produce and

put out into the world, you worry that you're inappropriate in some way, but you kind of don't care because you won't turn it off."

"...and I can't turn it off. And it's terrible music."

"That doesn't matter. In mine, it's pee, for crying out loud. You need it to be something terrible so you can test your ability to withstand the rejection for being inappropriate."

"But I don't even like this music! And I'm trying to turn it off the whole time!"

"Or are you... It is your iPod—it's coming from you."

"But it's not mine, I'm telling you. I can't even operate it."

"You know what we all worry about when we make art? We all worry about being terrible. You might, maybe, possibly be able to stop worrying for a few minutes about being good. But you never stop worrying about being terrible. The only thing worse than being terrible is not being heard in the first place."

Where the spirit cried out for the first time and was not heard. And where it will cry out for the last time and not be heard then, either. The little surface edges having sunken back down to the darkness and the dead. That's what Faulkner said. The only things saving us are the little noises we make to each other—the words, the syllables, the phonemes. The breath.

It's important enough to go back, I think, to Thanksgiving morning, 1996. My grad school friends and I all spent the night at Leah's house to get ready for the English department

potluck, which would no doubt, like all of the English department parties, start with too many chickpeas and end with
somebody being deemed offensive.

"I've got coffee already. It's in the bag with me. I'm waiting for Bullwinkle. Bullwinkle is the best." I answered Mona
from the living room. I had decided to remain in the sleeping
bag until I saw my favorite balloon. Or until cocktail hour.

"There is no Bullwinkle coming. You need to get past
this." Mona, no-nonsense, from the kitchen.

"Of course Bullwinkle is coming. I saw Bullwinkle in
person. He was reaching out for me, and I got scared that he
was going to fall on me, and I curled up in a ball and people
from New Jersey started yelling. I have a great debt to repay
to Bullwinkle, one day." Lying on the ground, you see, is the
story of my life.

"And how old were you when you transgressed against the
Monarch of the Glen?" Leah was writing about the Pre-
Raphaelites at the time.

"He's not a stag—he's a moose. I was eight."

"Come on, you know they retire those balloons. What are
you doing, standing there in your sleeping bag? You look like
a green intestine."

"No! She's Alice's caterpillar." Jamie bounced into the
living room and onto the sofa, playing along.

I pulled my head back into the sleeping bag, then bent
slowly toward the floor. Then I bent my elbows close together
and balanced my knees on them, then curled back up again to
the shape of a candy cane, turning slowly right and left. Mona
and Jamie were delighted, but Leah remained skeptical.

"Now that's just weird," she said, standing next to Mona at the kitchen bar with the coffee pot.

"I'm Mummenschantz," I announced. "Did you people emerge from the womb as grad students? Did no one have a childhood? Look! Snoopy. It's Snoopy!"

"Thank heavens. What an odd statistic: Katie Couric just said the parade is the second greatest annual consumer of helium in the United States."

"That's because she's number one, Leah. Mona, if you're waiting for the Foucault balloon, you're going to be disappointed. Sorry."

"His head would make a great balloon." Mona brightened.

"You all didn't actually have childhoods, did you?" Mine was a swamp, but punctuated with Mummenschantz and Bullwinkle, so it's all okay now.

"Has anyone ever been killed by one of those things?" Mona is both gloomy and risk-averse.

"Great. That's a statistic for Katie Couric. 'Since the parade's inception, fourteen bystanders have been killed by rampant cartoon replications, the greatest offender of which has been Winnie the Pooh, whose death toll of eight makes him the most prolific helium-based serial killer of all time. All tallied, forty-seven people have been killed by parade-related items, including floats, clowns, marching band instruments and the foot of one overzealous Rockette.'" I can, however, match or on occasion beat her at "grisly."

"Nobody dies at a parade. It's not allowed." Jamie is nicer than the rest of us, too nice even to know that she is. We are appropriately grateful, though.

Mona's not having it right this second, though. "Of course they do! There's all kinds of dangerous stuff around, and it's all in motion. AND there's huge crowds of people. It's like a war, just slower, and without clearly defined opposing sides."

"Well, there is a traditional connection. Parades and wars." I'm going somewhere with it.

"Anyway, if that were true, we'd just have parades every day." Leah's announcement is uncharacteristically random, so we all stop because we're trying to figure out what we missed.

But then the focus turned to me. I'd poked my head out of the end of the sleeping bag now and was standing at a deep slant to one side, like a leaning tower of asparagus.

"Nicole, what is it you're going for here, exactly? With your wardrobe choices, I mean."

"It's hard to be a parade all by yourself, Leah." They thought my wistful tone was meant to be ironic.

We'd spent all day Wednesday cooking the desserts: pies, cakes, an enormous banana pudding. It was fortunate that a cold front had come in so we could store some items in the garage that wouldn't fit in the refrigerator. Almost the whole department was coming—no one had time to go home with Christmas break so close and all those exams scheduled in between. Everyone was either taking them, grading them, or both. Hugh and Bonnie had dissertation defenses next week. We told people not to bother cooking—just to show up for a few hours. Everybody needed to eat, and to sleep in a turkey coma. Or a Tofurkey coma.

I wasn't going to be eating much that day. I'd been throwing up everything for a while. My whole body was sore—I ran into a friend a few days before on campus, and when he hugged me goodbye, I thought I could feel my insides cracking open and breaking apart. And Wednesday afternoon, when I spent about an hour peeling the hard-boiled eggs to devil them—the smell had driven me repeatedly to the backyard until I had to lie down on the ground. Mona had to come out and stand over me.

"Whatever it is, you're being more dramatic than usual. Are you very drunk? If so, it's impressive, because I haven't actually seen you drink anything."

She hadn't seen me, because I hadn't been drinking. "I'm not drunk," I moaned.

"Do you need to go to the hospital?"

"No."

"Do you need a bag?" Mona seemed to be sincere in her attempts to help.

"I'm outside. I'll just throw up into a bush."

"I mean, do you need a bag to breathe into?"

"Isn't that for hyperventilating?"

"Look, I'm no doctor but you're gray. It's freaking me out. I've never seen you like this."

"It's alright. Maybe it's food poisoning."

"Oh god, the eggs!"

"No, no. I'm sure the eggs are fine. Just give me a minute. Go back inside and I'll be in directly. Seriously. I'll be fine."

I had propped up on one side, leaning against the fence, to watch Mona look back over her shoulder at me in consternation as she opened the screen porch door. Then she disappeared into the house.

As near as I could tell, she just might have mentioned something about this episode to the rest of them at some point when I wasn't around. But nobody was being pushy. Just watching a little more than usual.

On the TV, there was a giant blue thing with spikes on its head floating down Fifth Avenue. So I redirected.

"What the fuck is that thing? What have they done with Bullwinkle?"

"That's Sonic the Hedgehog. Jeez, where was your childhood?" Mona chirped.

"Earlier than yours. That's no hedgehog. Mrs. Tiggy Winkle—that's a hedgehog. That's a… it kind of looks like a shoe."

"A shoe? It looks nothing like a shoe. Everything you don't like, you claim it resembles a shoe. If you're going to scorn, scorn with some sense at least. My word." Leah could say things like "my word" and sound neither prim nor ironic.

"Hey, you guys? I need to ask you a favor." I wasn't going to make it through the day. I couldn't mind-over-matter this one.

"What?" Jamie heard the turn in my voice first.

"I might die. I might have a tumor or something. I'm not sure." Was there a way to make this funny? Maybe not.

They stared.

"If this is an attempt at scorning with sense, it's not working."

"Either I'm going to die or I'm pregnant. Will one or all of you help me find an open drugstore? I don't think I can do this by myself."

"Of course. By the way, this is not increasing the level of sense. You don't date. You don't even own a sofa." Leah had been riding me about the absence of a damn sofa in my apartment. I felt like my failure at personal relationships had a deeper source than furniture, but I was willing to listen to suggestions, always.

"I'll drive." Mona looked relieved.

How many Humanities graduate students does it take to locate a pregnancy test in a drugstore?

No, still not funny.

"Well?" For some reason, they decided I should wait outside. They all came out looking a little pale and disturbed.

"I got one. Well, there's two in here, actually." Leah seemed to have taken the lead. Jamie smiled, her eyes a little moist. She carried the bag. Mona crossed her arms.

"That's good. If I only had one, I'm sure I'd drop it in the toilet. Or assume I'd misused it, no matter what the report." I said it, because it was true. I was really glad I had waited on the sidewalk, too.

"Of course, it would have taken less time without Mona having to wonder aloud and at great length about the uses of a product called Astroglide..." Leah looked at Mona with some frustration.

Mona unbundled her arms and shrugged in desperate appeal. "I'd just never heard of such a thing! Why would they call it that? Don't you wonder whether people actually listen to themselves?"

"Try not to wonder what most people are up to. It's dangerous terrain." Leah unlocked the car and we all got in and went back to the house, dangerously close to guest arrival time.

Around the kitchen table, they all agreed that another test could be interesting and useful, from a supporting-materials perspective, but that the initial result was sufficient.

"A plus sign will appear if... well, there you go." Leah had been reading the directions aloud.

"Yeah. That's emphatic." Mona seemed impressed.

Jamie hugged me. "Oh," she said, "I'm giving you a baby shower."

"Jeez, Jamie. She's not going to keep it. Are you?" Now Mona looked at me with round, startled eyes, all of the weight of this information seeming to bear down on her at once. Not always the most empathetic of this group, Mona's sorrow for me actually broke my own misery for a second. I wanted to comfort her.

That night, among the scholars, I pretended to drink as usual so that I could continue to claim things wildly and, as the evening got late enough, say things that were truly offensive.

CHAPTER THIRTY-THREE

SO YOU SEE, your timing was terrible. But I wanted you anyway. I had it figured out pretty fast—I don't even know that I figured anything. We knew each other from the start. The fact that I held on to your father after you were gone—I missed you. The whole thing was a surprise, yes. I thought I was going to die. But then, just as I saw what I realized I had been waiting for, it went by all of a sudden and was gone. I saw you coming, I recognized you, I waited for you and then I got it, I saw all of that beauty just as you went away. I knew you, but I never got to find out who you were. Nothing can ever tell me that in this world. Sometimes I see little pieces of it. But they only remind me of the thing I can't ever have.

I missed my Middle English final because I went out to California to tell your father I was pregnant. Making an art form out of shame, I avoided my professor until I got a distress email from him demanding to know whether or not I was okay. He had heard a variety of tales. I finally agreed to meet at his office.

I expressed my abject sorrow, not so much for missing the exam, but for bailing out completely and not even giving him an opportunity to discuss a plan with me.

"I found out on Thanksgiving that I was pregnant."

Dr. Barber was a sweet man with big, round, mischievous eyes. He had reportedly gone to graduate school with the members of Monty Python. The story always made me sad, because he was hilarious, but often at a level even his grad students couldn't follow. Or maybe they all suffered from that academic suspension of humor that afflicts so many.

Anyway, he struck me as lonely, and the separation from what was clearly his tribe made it worse.

"Oh my. And this is, not something you—"

"No. No indeed."

"And have you thought about—"

"That's what I was off doing. The father is in Los Angeles."

"OH."

His surprise was authentic. Almost no one could maintain any kind of relationship in graduate school that wasn't with another graduate student—which explained Dr. Barber's next question.

"UCLA?"

"No—he's actually not an academic. He's in the film industry."

Dr. Barber leaned back in his chair. "Oh! An actor? Or a writer? You write, am I correct? I knew this, I think."

"Yes. I mean, yes, I write, but no, he's not an actor. Now, he writes some, but that's not really—he's more of a—he's more on the production side of things—"

"Does he know, ah, the actress Drew Barrymore?"

I had to pause to let my brain catch up, because I wasn't expecting Barber to have a psychic moment, but I also didn't know where the Drew Barrymore pronouncement came from. Brad had just finished a movie with her and was currently kind of annoyed because the hotel had put all of her charges to his credit card, not hers. He explained that this kind of thing happened with famous people all the time—stores, hotels, restaurants got timid about using their credit card information even if it had been given expressly to them for that purpose. Like they were charging God for something. People thought if you were famous, you were untouchable and should not be charged for things like shoes and sandwiches.

"It's funny you should ask."

I had to spend an hour describing the movie that he'd be seeing in a theater the following year. But I got to take my exam. I wrote a film script based on *The Canterbury Tales* a few years back. As a kind of penance, I think. There's enough out of balance for me as it is.

I'm listening. I've been listening since that Thanksgiving, since it was not just me anymore and would never be only me again. Now there is always me and you. There is always us. I don't know where you are. But I can hear you. So hear me now: You stay with me. We aren't done yet. Tell those dogs to stop running. They're your dogs. You tell them what to do—they don't pull without your consent. And you tell them there's no more running anymore. Come in from the cold and settle down. You've been running for so long. Don't fight anymore. The air you've been trying to breathe is gone. If I could release you from all this myself, I'd do it. But I think you have to do it with me. We can make it stop. Just drop the reins. You have to let it go once and for all.

Wait a minute. Wait a minute. Is that right? What if I've had this whole thing backwards? I'm wrong about this. I've been wrong all along.

So, let me try again—I have been selfish. I didn't see it. I want to thank you for everything you did already. It was enough. Everything you already did was enough. I will be okay. You can go now. I love you. Thank you.

🗲

You can go now. I love you. Thank you.

CHAPTER THIRTY-FOUR

IT'S AS GOOD A DAY as any for a fact-checking mission. Not the library this time. A real live fact-checking mission. I'd have to decide just how many facts I was willing to give up myself in order to get the ones I needed. It was time to find out about the man in my house. Well, not exactly find out. I had already found out. I knew. I just wanted to know I knew. If you get me.

My driveway, it's not exactly blind, but you can't be tentative when you pull out. Even though there's a bunch of apartments no more than a mile away, my end of the road looks like the country, and the cars come speeding over the hill, never expecting to find anybody in their path. Pulling my coat tight against the icy wind—it was one of those days when the weather turned: it was warmer at 8 a.m. than it would be the rest of the day—I sprinted across, stopping just short of the ravine in front of the neighbor's side yard, the far corner of their property. Our closest neighbor was a geology professor at NC State. He came over right after we moved in and brought us an extensive report about the water table, the mineral content. I wasn't sure I could remember his name. The mailbox said Frank. Was that first or last? Last, I guessed.

"It's hard water," he'd said, handing over a folder full of charts and numbers. "But it's good water. You don't have to worry about any of the stuff you don't want in there. Run your own tests if you want. I do 'em about every six months. I'll let you know if I see anything significant."

"I love your house. Like the color," I had told him then. I did like the place, kind of a barn, painted dark green. It set down in the low land back from the road, nestled and hunched like a rabbit.

"Built it myself. Been here thirty-eight years. Most of us on this road have been here a long time. Not many people ever leave here. Once they move in."

"I understand the people who were in our house before us made some trouble in the neighborhood. Don't worry—we've got no plans to raise pit bulls, and our kids are pretty tame. Heh heh." Thomas had made a point of letting all the neighbors know that while we didn't know the previous owners, we had heard all the stories. We planned to stay a long time, too, and so we wanted to make a decent impression.

"That bastard cut all the old trees down by the road—that's what set everybody off to start with. We came to talk to him, and he said, 'They're my trees—I'll cut 'em all down if I want to.' We weren't sorry to see them go, I won't lie. Shitbird."

"Then that guest house burning down…"

"Yeah. Strange. Wasn't it."

He was on his way out already by then, but he stopped on our front porch and looked at me over his shoulder. "Guest house. Party house, more like."

Thomas laughed. "Yeah, I think you're right. I've found a lot of beer cans down in the woods, cleaning up."

"Nothing you find in those woods would surprise me."

That was the only time I'd seen him to talk. Once in a while, his big Chevy pickup would be lumbering out of his driveway while I was coming in or out. I guess he could take his time, because if anybody hit him, he'd do more damage than they would.

Safely out of the street, I walked up the steep driveway, watching the house rise up out of the ground—first the peaked roof, then the shutters of the second floor windows with X-shapes like barn doors. Then the full view of the house to its foundation, its green exterior that would blend in completely with the grove of trees around it when the summer came. In the winter, it looked like Sleeping Beauty's castle caught in its thicket of briars, everyone inside asleep. That is, if her castle had been a really nice barn.

Knocking for the third time, I was about to leave when I saw him peeking around the side of the house.

"Hey. You're the new neighbor."

"We been there three years—uh, yeah, the 'new' neighbor. Hey. Have you got a minute? Sorry to come over unannounced."

"Don't worry about it. I was in the shed. You're lucky. I came out to take a whiz."

The nature of my luck was multifold, it seemed.

"I just wanted to ask you something. It's about our house. I figured you'd know the answers, since you've been here a long time. It won't take but a few minutes if you don't mind."

"I don't mind. It's a good house. Good water. Well-situated on that rise. If your basement ever floods, you better start lining up the animals two-by-two, because the end of the damn world is coming."

"My husband says that very same thing all the time."

"Hm. Stay right there."

He disappeared around the corner. The same spiders who'd laid siege to our porch were laying into his. It looked like he might have conceded at least this region to them. I saw one of those funnel webs you usually only see in horror movies with giant arachnids or pod people.

Staring at the funnel web, my insides were calculating again. Maybe it was just the creepy spider webs, but something was churning up. I could feel the static on me. I didn't know what it was, though—I couldn't get a who yet, but something about Frank's house had a lot of bound-up energy. It was hard to tell, good or bad. I always hated the word "liminal" in grad school: it was the sauce everything got basted in for about a hot second in 1994. But I was on a literal threshold. Not just with the spiders.

Finally, after a pretty good amount of clanking and sliding, the door swung open.

"I've been robbed," he announced, stepping aside and waving me in.

"Oh, wow. Oh, holy shit." The first exclamation was for his announcement, but the second came at the sight of an enormous owl—that sucker had about a four-foot wingspan— that perched just inside his doorway, swooping out of a deep shadow.

"Not today. Four times, though. That's just Mabel. She's dead. You don't have to duck."

"I guess the thieves came in the back way."

"Now that you mention it..."

"Maybe you should put something scarier back there."

"I did."

"Okay then. Thanks for letting me in the front."

"My wife died. Then my dog died. Then I got robbed four times. Not enough eyes on the place anymore."

Mabel wasn't the only dead bird in the house. And that was only one link of the food chain. There were squirrels, foxes, something that looked like a tiny mountain lion, and what might've been a groundhog. A lot of deer heads. A hairy pig thing with tusks. Pinned-down snakes, bugs and butterflies.

"We're in a little pocket, you know, right here between the campus and the highway. All the student housing up that way," he said, waving to the south, "and all the plastic horse-shit up that way," to the west, where the fast food restaurants and convenience stores were. "Nobody told 'em it was time to move. They just got trapped one day. Now they're here forever. They can't get out of here. Got nowhere to go if they did. Keep building this shit everywhere."

"Looks like a few of 'em might have ended up in your living room."

"There's too damn many deer. They eat everything, then the other animals die. I just keep the predators in check. Sometimes I take care of the injured ones." Frank rested his hand on the arched back of a weasel on a side table.

I walked along the side of the room, scanning the framed maps, geological studies, antlers, glass jars of eyeballs. "Don't get me wrong. I don't have a problem with it. I see what you mean about the deer—I like them, and they were here on this land before I was, but they scare the crap out of my dog. Early one morning last week, my daughter ended up nose-to-nose with a giant buck. She was taking out the trash before we left for school. He was right up at the trash cans."

"I know him. It's the season, you know. Watch out for 'em.

They can hurt that little one you got over there, not even realize it. Watch that hawk, too. Got any cats?"

"Allergic." I wasn't, but Thomas was.

"Just as well. That hawk'll fly off with anything smaller than a beagle."

I had gotten distracted by the drawings on his far wall, bird after bird, including the tiny blue ones I'd never seen before moving here. All of these drawings—the big gray-and-yellow ones, the fat cardinals the size of poultry—I'd seen all these birds in my yard. And those brown spiders. The tiny bugs that looked like helmets with feet. They were all there, labeled and detailed.

"Oh, hey, I got interested in your drawings and I almost forgot. It's not really a big deal, but I was just wondering if you could tell me anything about, if you knew anything about... did you know the man who lived in our house? Did he build it?"

"You mean Bert? Herbert? The first owner. Before those people added on to it."

"That's right. The first one. In 1967. Did Bert build the house himself?"

"He did a lot of it. He had somebody lay the foundation and frame it out, you know. But Bert was there for every bit. And he hung a lot of the drywall himself. Did a lot of the wiring. Did all the finishing work, made the kitchen cabinets out back in his shed. Probably took him longer, but it was solid construction, not like today. They didn't have much money, but Bert loved that house."

"Oh, yeah. I know. I mean, I figured. It's a good house."

He looked at me a little funny for a second, I thought. I thought I saw something, anyway.

"Bert was a good guy. Quiet, but that never bothered me. Not one for a lot of chatter myself."

"Well, I don't want to take too much of your time. I appreciate the information. Just one more thing—what happened to Bert? Did he sell the house?"

He shifted his weight from one foot to the other and scratched the back of his neck. "Naw. Bert didn't sell the house."

I'd made him uncomfortable now. But his reaction was exactly as I'd expected, somehow, even as my heart sped up watching him.

"You don't have to say anymore. Sounds like it might've been—"

"No, no, it's not—he didn't lose it to the bank or anything like that. His kid inherited it. Kid was kind of a prick."

I hadn't really been thinking that, but I can understand how for Frank here that might be the saddest version of a story about a house.

"It's pretty simple, really. He was out in his shed, working on some piece of furniture or trimwork, like usual. His wife just found him out there. The firemen got here first. I thought the place was on fire when I came out here and looked across the street."

He stopped and took out a pair of round eyeglasses, polishing them with the corner of his flannel shirt.

"Tell you the truth, I don't know if he died right there or after they took him to the hospital. I'm not even sure if it was a heart attack or a stroke. I never asked. He was out there working, like he liked to be. He never would have wanted to be anyplace else. Built some beautiful pieces. Cabinetry. Things like you can't hardly find now. Hardly had to use a nail—all handmade joinery."

"But he was pretty young? I mean, not old or anything."

"He was probably sixty-five or so. Young to me now, not then. I've already told my kids—I get too old to live in this house by myself, you just take me out to the shed and put me down. Stuff me and prop me up if you want. But don't leave me half alive somewhere I can't swing a hammer."

"Or stuff a bat." We looked at each other, both of us with our hands stuffed deep into our pockets, squared off in a room full of dead critters. "It's a really great bat. I like it."

"That one didn't come from around here. I've had that one for years. Caught in in my daddy's barn one Christmas."

"It's fine work." I wasn't sure how to compliment taxidermy, it occurred to me. Overly flowery praise seemed inappropriate. But I was taken with the bat.

"It was the first one I was proud of."

What a thing to say, I thought.

"The first thing you make that you're proud of. That means a lot."

Frank was digging some dust or something out of the weasel's ear. He didn't look up. "Yep. 'Cause you never know which one's the last one you're gonna be proud of."

I got to thinking about what Bert might have been building back there in the shed that day. If I'd been his wife, or his daughter, would I be keeping a half-finished piece of sculpture in my house? A two-legged table, or a chest with no drawers. See, I wouldn't have changed a thing. Maybe that's the trouble.

"Bert's shed. Was it back there where that foundation is? Where the... party house burned down?"

"Let me see. Round about fifty yards from your garage door, northwest toward the big road." He squinted and held up his hand as if he could see past the front walls of his living room, up the hill, across the street and into my yard.

"Behind that line of pine trees they brought in to try to divide the property."

"That's about right. I think that's about right where it was. Hadn't really thought about it before. But I'm pretty sure. Yeah." He nodded and patted his own cheek, as if incidental. "Struck by lightning."

"What?" I thought I might have misunderstood him.

"That damn house of card-playin' no-good sons of bitches. They tried to blame it on me, but I saw it. They were out of town and we had one of those four o'clock summer blowouts, big old electrical storm. I lost a few trees myself. Maybe that's why it took me a few extra minutes to call the fire department."

"You saw it? When it got hit?"

Frank had the weasel tucked up under his arm now. He stared down at it, lost in thought. "This one. I can't ever get him quite right. Damn thing still looks cross-eyed."

"I should be getting home. Back to Bert's house."

He looked up and smiled slyly at me then.

"Is it still Bert's house?"

I thought a little about how to answer Frank on this point.

"I'm pretty sure it is. What do we ever get to know for sure in this world?"

"Oh, you're a philosopher, then." Frank sounded disappointed in me.

"I surely hope not."

"Use what you got, young lady. Do me a favor and say hello to Bert."

"Don't spook me, now."

"I'll say it again—Bert was a good guy." He raised one hand a little, half blessing, half salute.

"It's a good house. He should be proud. I hope he likes what we've done with the place. Sometimes I worry—"

"You've got nothing to worry about. False alarm."

Yes. That's what it was.

On my way back toward the road, I saw my own house reappear over the hill, bits at a time. I crossed under the heavy buzzing of the power lines running down past the city greenway, past the curve of the road. I felt better. I hadn't had any expectations, and I learned more from my neighbor than he knew that I did. Specifics weren't even on the table right now.

All I needed for today was to know that I could listen, that I could hear. It doesn't make sense to be sitting there all your life waiting for your favorite song to play when you don't even have the radio on, when you don't even try to find a station. I'd keep lighting a candle. Keep saying hello to Bert.

But maybe there was one more important thing.

"Hello?"

There was a Bojangles box and a pair of pantyhose in the ditch next to the driveway. The stories are everywhere, I swear. I stood on the edge of my land and called them out one more time for the day, because it was time I showed them the property lines.

"Okay. All right. I know this might not be the right time or place or whatever. I'm not feeling especially in touch with my third eye or my root chakra. And I don't have any of those fancy meters or gadgets or talking boxes like they do on TV. But I know you can hear me, and I want to get a couple of things straight with you. All of you."

If you don't let people know what you expect from them, they'll run right over you.

Dead or alive, it's the same. Not to sound like a self-help book.

"First of all, don't interrupt me when I'm doing something important. Important things include stuff like driving the car or attending a parent-teacher meeting. Oh, and you're going to get a much better response if you come around after coffee or before whiskey."

Manners. That's all I'm talking about here.

"Second: Do not scare the children. Or the dog, if you can manage it. Just have a little consideration, okay? Ask yourself, am I being threatening?"

Okay then. I don't think that's unreasonable.

"One more thing, in that arena. I don't want to see you, do you hear me? No physical manifestations. I hear you, right? Message received? Don't show yourselves. I'm in no mood. Just... don't."

I did want to be fair.

"We can revisit that third rule later. But for now, no visuals. That means you, gray lady. Look, in the meantime, I'll do my best to pay attention. Bert, I know you're there every time I turn on the blender. Maybe you were a Margarita man. Maybe I'll go visit Frank again sometime and find out."

And then I could ask about the upstairs back bedroom. And the patch of woods by the road. This case is... open-ended. Well, at least, it's not too late. It's probably never too late. Probably. It's only, what? Thursday? Thursday. Nobody starts or stops anything on a Thursday.

"Like I said, manners matter, living or dead."

A car passes behind me. I don't see it, just feel the strong cold draft of air push me roughly toward the trees, the yard, toward home. Above me, a snow-sky not ready for snow. Nora's left the window open. She's playing music in her room. I can hear it, little pieces of melody I almost understand, a transmission coming to me through the branches.

↯

PUBLISHER'S AFTERWORD

I published Nicole's first book over a decade ago, when she could still write a poem that rhymed, you know, when she still had it together. That said, *Karate Bride* was a very odd book, full of strange stories—all of them true, even the one about me.

When she called me about this work, she explained that she "was tired of acting normal," and that somehow publishing this book would help. It took reading about a half page before I understood what she meant.

I told her I figured that the only way we could publish this and keep her out of the nut house (much less let her keep her job) was to change a couple of names and call it a novel.

So hey folks—this book is a novel. That happens to have some 'Occasionally True' stories. All the truly strange stuff is totally made up. Yep.

Phil Bevis
Publisher, Chatwin Books

About the Author

Nicole Sarrocco, the author of this *Occasionally True* series of novels, lives in Raleigh, North Carolina with her husband and two children. Raised on a tobacco farm on the Wake-Johnston County line, she has a PhD in English, and loves teaching high school. She never has pretended to be normal, but does claim that good manners are in her regional DNA.

CPSIA information can be obtained at www.ICGtesting.com
Printed in the USA
LVOW07s1629121115

462271LV00007B/637/P

9 781633 980006